Moses, Me, and Murder

Moses, Me, and Murder

A Barkerville Mystery
from the author of *By the Skin of His Teeth*
and *The Doctor's Apprentice*

Ann Walsh

DUNDURN
TORONTO

Editor: Michael Carroll
Copy-editor: Laura Harris
Design: Courtney Horner
Printer: Webcom

Library and Archives Canada Cataloguing in Publication

Walsh, Ann, 1942-
        Moses, me and murder : a Barkerville mystery / Ann Walsh.

Issued also in electronic formats.
ISBN 978-1-4597-0967-6

        I. Title.

PS8595.A585M6 2013   jC813'.54   C2013-900781-4

1   2   3   4   5   17   16   15   14   13

Conseil des Arts   Canada Council
du Canada   for the Arts

Canada

ONTARIO ARTS COUNCIL
CONSEIL DES ARTS DE L'ONTARIO

We acknowledge the support of the **Canada Council for the Arts** and the **Ontario Arts Council** for our publishing program. We also acknowledge the financial support of the **Government of Canada** through the **Canada Book Fund** and **Livres Canada Books**, and the **Government of Ontario** through the **Ontario Book Publishing Tax Credit** and the **Ontario Media Development Corporation**.

Care has been taken to trace the ownership of copyright material used in this book. The author and the publisher welcome any information enabling them to rectify any references or credits in subsequent editions.

                                                                                    J. Kirk Howard, President

Printed and bound in Canada.

Visit us at
Dundurn.com | Definingcanada.ca | @dundurnpress | Facebook.com/dundurnpress

Visit Ann Walsh at www.annwalsh.ca

Cover photo is of the noted Canadian actor, Alvin Sanders, who portrayed Moses on the streets of Barkerville for many years. *Photo credit Ron Young, photographer.*

Dundurn	Gazelle Book Services Limited	Dundurn
3 Church Street, Suite 500	White Cross Mills	2250 Military Road
Toronto, Ontario, Canada	High Town, Lancaster, England	Tonawanda, NY
M5E 1M2	LA1 4XS	U.S.A. 14150

This book is for
Katherine and Megan
and
all the other Cariboo children past, present, and future.

Contents

The Stranger | 9

Moses and Me | 13

He Returns | 20

Moses's Story: The Face of Luck | 26

A Dilemma | 31

News! | 35

Captured! | 41

The Clue | 46

Murderer on the Loose! | 54

The Journey | 61

At the Bridge | 66

We Return | 71

Interlude | 75

The Trial | 79

The Other Side of the Story | 84

The Verdict | 89

A Life for a Life | 92

It Ends – Perhaps | 97

Acknowledgements | 101

Historical Notes | 103

Characters | 105

Blessing's Grave | 109

1

The Stranger

The door to the barbershop flew open so hard that it banged back against the wall. Standing in the entrance, scowling, was a tall, heavily bearded man. He made me nervous, although he was just standing there, staring at Moses. I consider myself as brave as any other twelve-year-old boy, but this man looked — threatening — somehow. I sat down quietly on a bench and pretended I wasn't there.

"Moses!" the stranger said, "I hear tell you've been looking for me."

"No, suh, Mistuh Barry, suh! I been looking for my chum, Mr. Charles Blessing. As I recall, suh, you and I weren't so friendly that I'd go out of my way looking for you!"

I knew that Moses was upset. He always uses that slow, southern drawl with lots of "suh's" when he is angry or worried. Moses comes from Victoria, and he usually speaks as well as any other man in Barkerville. Better than most of the miners.

"I heard tell that you was looking for me, Moses!" The tall stranger slammed the door and strode into the shop. "Well, here I am. What do you want?"

Moses is a small man, not much over five feet, and very slightly built. Almost skinny. He didn't move away, but stood still, looking up at the stranger, his face empty of expression.

"I asked if anyone seen *Mr. Blessing*, suh, not you. Now that you're here maybe you can tell me where he is. I'm remembering the two of you left Quesnel together. Now you're here in Barkerville, and he can't be found. Do you know where he is, suh?"

The stranger took a step backwards, his big, rough hands pulling at his beard. "Why — why I left Blessing behind me on the road. He had sore feet; couldn't keep up. Haven't seen hide nor hair of him since Quesnel."

Moses turned his back, and became very busy rearranging bottles of hair tonic, the special hair invigorator that he alone knows how to make. "He didn't say anything to me about having sore feet," he said quietly.

"Well, he did," Barry snarled. "And I ain't seen him, so quit your nosing around and asking questions. I ain't seen him since I left him behind me on the road. I'm not the man's keeper."

He turned and stomped out, slamming the door behind him.

"Moses? Who was that?"

Moses stopped fussing with the bottles of hair restorer. "That was James Barry," he said. "I met him in Quesnel, on my way back from Victoria in May."

"Why was he so upset?" I don't normally ask a lot of questions, especially not of adults. They give you such strange answers if they don't like what you're asking. But Moses was different. He was my friend. So, I went on.

"What was Mr. Barry so mad for? And who is this Mr. Blessing that you were talking about?"

"He's someone I met on the journey back to Barkerville, long before I met Barry. Charles Blessing and I travelled together for a while, sharing grub and campfires."

"But, Moses ..." I began.

He interrupted, "It wasn't until Quesnel that we met Barry. I had to stay on to see about some money owed me and couldn't leave for a while. But Charles didn't want to wait for me to finish my business. He decided to travel on the next day with his new companion — Barry."

He paused. "You know, Ted, it's a funny thing. Charles Blessing said that he wasn't sure he should go on with Barry. Didn't trust him, somehow. But he was in a hurry. Wanted to get to Williams Creek and strike rich before his money ran out.

"Charles didn't care much for Barry, though. He told me to remember that his full name was Charles Morgan Blessing, and that he came from Ohio. He said he felt sort of uneasy, and if anything happened to him, I at least, would know who he was."

"Where is Mr. Blessing, Moses?"

"I don't know, Ted. I was only one day behind them out of Quesnel and I should have caught up with them somewhere in Barkerville by now. But I haven't seen Charles since the end of May, the day before he and Barry were to leave for the gold fields. Now it's almost August.

"I've asked all around, too. No one in town has seen a newcomer named Charles Blessing."

"What made Mr. Barry so angry? All you were doing was asking about your friend."

"I don't know, Ted. I just don't know. Maybe we'll find out one of these days."

We did find out — but I wish we hadn't.

2

Moses and Me

As I walked home that afternoon through the busy streets of Barkerville, I thought about Moses and me. We'd become friends over a year ago, shortly after my family had come to the Williams Creek area. My hair needed cutting and Ma had heard that Moses was the best barber around. One afternoon she hustled me off to see him.

Unfortunately, I didn't feel that I needed a haircut, and I guess I was complaining a lot because, as I sat down in the barber's chair, Ma suddenly exploded. "Theodore Percival MacIntosh! Close your mouth and mind your manners. I'll see you later, young man, and Mr. Moses better have a good report on your behaviour!" She stormed out to do some shopping at Mason and Daly's general store, just up the street.

"Theodore, eh?" said Moses as he went to work with the scissors.

"Um," I agreed, hardly opening my mouth.

"Percival, eh?" said Moses.

"Um," I said again, beginning to squirm. I hate my name. It's too long and fancy. At school, back in New

Westminster, they used to call me Percy, just to make me mad. It did.

"Theodore — Percival — MacIntosh, eh?" repeated Moses. "Well, I could have guessed the MacIntosh part. This red hair, all those freckles, and your green eyes show a Scottish ancestor somewhere behind you. But you don't look much like a Theodore Percival!" Then he began to laugh.

I swirled around in the chair. "It's *not* funny! How would you like to go through life with the longest, stupidest name anyone ever had?"

"Oh, a touch of a fine Scots temper, too, I see!" Moses laughed softly, as he went back to cutting my hair. "The point is, son, that I *have* gone through life with the longest, stupidest name anyone ever had. Or at least for fifty years. My full name is Wellington Delaney Moses! Mighty big name for the little fellow I turned out to be, don't you think?"

"Wellington Delaney Moses?" I said slowly. Then I grinned. "Nope. I think my name is dumber."

"Nonsense, young man! Mine is longer."

We looked at each other in the mirror and smiled. That was the beginning of the friendship. When Ma came back for me, I was perched on a bench in one corner of the shop with Moses beside me, listening as he told me stories of my new town. The barbershop is right across the street from Barnard's Express Company, and when he isn't busy, Moses sits and watches the stagecoaches arrive and leave. He knew who came into town and who left, whether they were happy or sad, and often just why they were travelling. There wasn't much going on in Barkerville in 1866 that Moses didn't know, or couldn't make a good guess about. He saw the hurdies, the dancing girls, arrive, welcomed by a cheering crowd of miners; he saw Judge Begbie, the Hanging Judge, leave after the trials had ended. He watched the hopeful newcomers, their faces glowing with the thought of the gold waiting for them on the banks of Williams Creek, step wonderingly off the stage. Often he saw those same men, their money exhausted and their hopes dashed, climb back onto the stage a few months later, heading for home and their old lives. Williams Creek did not smile favourably on everyone who came to seek her gold. Only one man in a hundred ever struck it rich. The rest — well, Moses knew the sad stories as well as the happier ones. He knew of Billy Barker who found his mother lode fifty-two feet down; a claim so rich that the town was named for him. He had met Cariboo Cameron, who found his wealth but lost his wife to "mountain fever," sometimes called typhoid, one of the deadliest of the illnesses that flourishes in the gold fields.

Rich or poor, success or failure, happy, sad, drunk, destitute, or content — Moses knew them all.

Ma could hardly drag me away from the barbershop that first day. Moses invited me to come back and visit. I did. The very next day, and almost every day since.

Moses remembers everything that goes on, partly because he keeps a diary telling who arrives or leaves on the stage. He also writes about the weather, so if anyone in town has a dispute about when the first snow fell last year, or which winter was the coldest, Moses can bring out his journals and settle the argument.

On my way home that day, the day I first saw James Barry in the barbershop, I stuck my head into my pa's carpentry shop to see if he was finished and wanted to walk home with me. He still had work to do, however, as he had promised one of Madame Bendixen's dancing girls that her new commode would be ready by morning. I went on alone.

Although Pa's shop is almost in the centre of Barkerville, right on the main street, we don't live near it. Our home is about a half mile from Barkerville, on the road to Richfield. Ma didn't want to live right in town. There were so many saloons, so many drunken miners and so much noise that, after only two nights in the Nicol Hotel, she started pressuring Pa to find a quieter place to live.

"Theodore needs a home where quiet and dignity have a place," she said. "I will not have him listening to that rough language on the street night after night!"

As soon as we could, we moved away from the busy town. Our home was about halfway between Barkerville and Richfield. Prices and rents are cheaper up there, but the road is uphill all the way — and steep! Then, of course, it's downhill all the way coming back to Barkerville, so I guess I can't complain.

I suppose Ma found her quiet and dignity. She sure makes me be quiet enough when I'm doing my lessons. There isn't a school in Barkerville, or anywhere near the Creek. There aren't enough children for one. I kicked up my heels and whooped a bit when I found that out, but Ma had other ideas. "Three hours a day with your nose in the books, Theodore. Three hours a day!" Unfortunately, there is a library in Barkerville, so she never runs out of books.

And she found a music teacher! So, on top of all the studying, I have to spend an hour a day practicing the violin. It's almost worse than regular school, even though Mr. Malanion is very understanding. He used to play the violin in the Paris Opera, and sometimes, if I'm having trouble with a piece, he'll tell me to put my violin away while he takes his out. Then he plays some of the most wonderful music I have ever heard. It almost makes me want to cry; other times the music is so cheerful that I want to laugh.

"You'll see, Ted, you'll see," he'll say as he puts his violin away. "It will be worth it in the end. Believe me."

On those days I go home feeling very ambitious, and practice until my fingers ache. I guess I still don't sound much like Mr. Malanion, though.

Well, I'd had no music lesson today. Only a visit with Moses and a meeting with that strange James Barry. I was beginning to feel hungry as I reached Barkerville's Chinatown. Unfamiliar aromas drifted out of the stores and cabins, mixing with the smell of dust and manure from the road.

I went by Sing Kee's store. Mr. Kee sells herbs — all kinds of herbs to cure you or make you feel good. His store is a dark, mysterious looking place with bunches of dried plants and roots and other things hanging from the ceiling, and lots of tiny, coloured bottles all around. I want to go in someday and see if he has something that will take my wart away, but Ma has absolutely forbidden it.

At last I was out of Barkerville; the fancier houses, hotels and saloons had given way first to Chinatown and now to simple miner's shacks. Our house isn't exactly a shack, but it isn't anything like the big home we had on the coast. I don't mind because I can hear the creek running nearby all summer. The little jays we call whiskey jacks and the squirrels come and beg for crumbs. Our new home has things you could never get in New Westminster.

I was getting tired. The road was steep, and the sky had become dark. By the looks of things, another sudden thunderstorm was on its way. I knew how heavy those August rains could be, so I began to hurry.

Suddenly I shivered, and it wasn't just because of the drop in temperature that the clouds had brought. I had the feeling that someone was watching me, someone I couldn't see but who could see me very well. The hairs on the back of my neck prickled and goosebumps stood on my arms.

I whirled around. No one was on the road behind me. There was no one under the trees that lined the road beside me, either. I shrugged my shoulders, beginning to whistle as I increased my speed. I could have sworn that someone was looking at me, someone who meant me no good. The feeling was so strong that, again, I looked behind me. Nothing.

I kept walking, even faster now. Suddenly a dark figure stepped out from behind a tree on the path ahead of me. I jumped, but kept whistling and walking. Then, as I got closer, I recognized him. It was the man who had been in Moses's shop that afternoon — James Barry!

The whistle died away. My throat was dry and I couldn't purse my lips properly. Barry stood, waiting and watching, as I drew closer to him. Taking a deep breath and lifting my hat, carelessly I hoped, I bid him a good evening.

"Master Theodore MacIntosh, eh?" He stepped out in front of me, blocking the trail. "Or is it Master Percy? What were you doing in Moses's shop? What's he to you, anyway?"

I was startled. How did he know who I was? Why was he asking about Moses? And where did he learn my name, even my middle name?

I didn't want to speak to him at all, but Ma has very strict rules about being polite to adults. I couldn't just ignore his questions, even though he made me feel very uneasy.

"Moses is my friend, sir," I said, trying to keep my voice from trembling. What was wrong with me? Why should I be afraid of this stranger, someone I had only just met?

"I often visit with Moses," I went on, "and now, if you'll excuse me, I seem to be late for dinner."

With that my courage deserted me. I pushed past him and ran up the trail as fast as I could. It wasn't very dignified, but I didn't feel very dignified. I felt scared for no particular reason, but scared just the same.

Behind me I could hear James Barry laughing. It was a deep laugh, a most unpleasant one, and it carried clearly up the trail.

"Well, Master Percy," he called after me. "We'll have to see what we can do about you!"

3

He Returns

The weeks went by. August slipped into September and the leaves became golden and brown. Williams Creek seemed to be running more strongly now, as if it knew that thick ice would soon lock it away for the winter. I hadn't seen any robins for weeks; they and the swallows had left for some warmer place. At night you could see your breath in the moonlight, and in the morning the sun burnt off a thin glaze of frost. Winter comes early to the gold fields.

I was in Moses's shop when that man, James Barry, came in again. I hadn't seen him since the day on the road to Richfield when he had frightened me so much. Hadn't bothered to ask where he was, either!

"Well, Moses. How about a haircut and a trim?"

"Certainly, suh. Regular rates, you understand."

As Moses settled Barry in the barber's chair, I looked around me. Maybe I could sneak out the door ...

Too late. Barry had seen me. "If it isn't my friend, Master MacIntosh," he said, his strong teeth flashing beneath his dark beard. "I haven't seen you for a while, young man.

Not since you took your abrupt departure from me on the Richfield road." He threw back his head and laughed.

"Not thinking of taking your departure again, are you Master Theodore? Or is it Master Percy?"

"I have errands to do for my mother," I lied, standing up and heading for the door.

"Sit down Master Percy. Stay a while." He laughed again. He had the meanest sounding laugh I'd ever heard.

I sank back onto the bench. I could think of a dozen places I'd rather be — in the woodshed waiting for a licking, at school, anywhere — but I saw no way of leaving without offending Mr. Barry. And that was something I didn't want to do.

Moses was busy cutting Barry's hair now. By the look on his face I guessed it was none too clean.

"You've been doing all right by yourself, suh," he commented. "Judging by the fancy clothes you're wearing, I'd say you must have hit pay dirt somewhere. As I recollect, you didn't have any money coming into Barkerville, so I guess the town has been good to you."

"I look after myself, Moses, I look after myself. And I keep my ears open, too. Hear all kinds of interesting things if you keep your ears open, you know. Like certain young whippersnapper's middle names." He laughed again. "You might say that Barkerville's been good to me, real good."

Barry *was* well dressed. His clothes, unlike his hair, looked clean and fresh. A gold watch fob hung along his vest, and a brand new hat lay where he had placed it on a table. His boots, too, were not the boots of a hard-working miner, but seemed more like the boots of a gambler

— or a man who had struck it rich. They also looked new, the leather gleaming in the dim light of the store. In his coat lapel he wore a large stickpin. The pin had been made from a gold nugget, a *very* large nugget!

Moses, too, had caught sight of the nugget. From where he stood, above and behind Barry as he tended to his hair, he could see it upside-down.

"Barry!" Moses's voice was suddenly harsh, as if he had been surprised by something. "Where did you get that nugget?"

Barry turned slowly, deliberately, to stare at Moses. "I brought it with me from California," he said quietly. "What business is it of yours, anyway?"

"None, suh. I was just going to say that it surely is a large and unusual piece of gold."

"You wouldn't be thinking you'd seen it somewhere before?"

"No, suh! Positively not, suh! I never saw that gold nugget anywhere in my life before!"

Moses was doing his trick with the southern accent, very strongly. I sat up straighter, wondering what had made him so upset.

Moses abruptly picked up a bottle of his hair restorer. "Can I interest you in a treatment of my own Hair Invigorator, suh? Absolutely free and on the house. I guarantee the restoration of any lost hair in one week, and a softer and fuller head of hair. If you would care to see signed statements from satisfied customers, I can produce several for your ..."

"Shut up!" Barry lowered his voice. "I don't want any Hair Invigorator. Do my beard now and hurry up."

It didn't take Moses long to finish trimming Barry's beard. He seemed worried, though, and I noticed that his hands were shaking as he worked.

Barry stood up, settled his bill, and turned to go. At the door he stopped, turning around to face Moses.

"About that nugget. It's a good thing you ain't seen it before. It's mine; always has been and always will be. I wouldn't want people to be talking otherwise now, would I? And if they do talk, Moses, if they do talk, I'll know who's been telling tales, won't I?" He smiled, looking directly at me.

"Master Percy here's a good friend of yours, isn't he, Moses? Leastwise, that's what I hear from people who know all about him. Would be an awful shame if something were to happen to him, right when he's in the pride of his youth. We wouldn't want anything unfortunate to happen to Master Percy now, would we?"

Moses hurried across the room to stand by my side. He put an arm around me. "No suh, Mistuh Barry. I ain't ever seen that nugget before and I ain't going to talk to no one! Please go now. Get out of my shop!"

Barry left, laughing his strange laugh. We watched him go.

"What was all of that about, Moses?" I asked. "He sounded almost as if he were threatening me."

"Don't you worry your head about Mister Barry," said Moses. "He won't touch you. I'll see to that! I won't say anything!"

"Won't say anything about what?"

"Never you mind, Ted. That's grown-up business and I'll tend to it. Never you mind."

"Oh, Moses, you've told me lots of grown-up stories before, some I wouldn't dare tell my mother. Why can't you tell me now?"

Moses sat down in the barber's chair. He didn't look well. His normally deep black skin had gone a funny shade, almost grey, and his eyes were glassy. I went to him.

"Are you all right? Can I get you a glass of water, or some of that medicine you keep in the cupboard?"

"How do you know about my heart tonic?" Moses forgot to be upset for a moment. Then he smiled. "You surely are a noticing young man. But no, thank you, Ted. I'll be all right."

He shut his eyes and leaned back against the chair's headrest. After a few minutes he seemed almost to have forgotten that I was there, for he began to mutter to himself. "What to do, what to do now? Can't take a chance on him harming the boy. Yet Charles was my friend. What to do, what to do?"

I went to him and put my hand on his arm. "Moses? What is it? You can tell me."

He jumped. He had forgotten about me. "Ted? Run along home now, run along."

"Nope. I'm not going until you tell me what's the matter."

"I can't tell you, Ted. Please, just go home."

"If you won't tell me what's so upsetting about that nugget Mr. Barry's wearing, I'm going to go to Constable Sullivan. I'll tell him that something peculiar is going on. He'll get the truth from you!"

"Theodore! That's blackmail!"

"Blackmail or not, I'm not going anywhere until you tell me the whole story."

I should have kept my mouth shut as Ma's always telling me. Moses did tell me the story, all of it. Now I'm scared, really scared. And now there's two of us in Barkerville who don't know what to do.

4

Moses's Story: The Face of Luck

No one came into the barbershop as Moses told me his story. No one came in, and even the street outside, usually so noisy, grew still — almost as if it were listening. I sat on the bench, not moving. As Moses spoke it almost seemed as if the shop and Barkerville faded away. I felt as if I, too, were out on the trail, coming into the gold fields on foot, coming to search for my fortune, for a new life.

"You see, Ted," Moses said. "I first met Charles Blessing in New Westminster. We were both alone, so we decided to travel together. A little company along the way makes the miles seem shorter. He was a good companion — generous with his money, easy to talk to, to laugh with. I guess you might say that by the time we reached the Junction we were friends, good friends.

I was going home to Barkerville. I'd closed my shop there and gone to Victoria for the winter. My friends and some of my family are in Victoria; I've only been in the Cariboo for a few years. You know, Ted, the long winters in this country can be hard on a man, hard on his body and on his soul. So, I'd taken some time off, gone back to a milder climate.

By May, though, I figured Williams Creek would be thawed and the sun would be warm during the day, even if the nights were still cold. I decided to come back to the gold fields. I'd picked up a lot of good stories on the coast, and I reckoned I could give my customers a pretty entertaining time when I got home. Also, I planned to expand the barbershop's merchandise. I invested in specialty items for the ladies. You know, fancy lace handkerchiefs, the new style button boots, velvet ribbons — some of the little luxuries women can't find in Barkerville. I figured I would make a lot of money when I began selling the stuff, but it had cost me plenty to buy it. It had already been shipped and was waiting for me in the Cariboo. Right then, though, I was, shall we say, a little short of ready cash. That's why I was doing the trip on foot instead of by stagecoach and steamer. Actually, by May I was as near broke as I'd ever been in my life, and tired to death of eating bannock and beans. I began to cut hair and trim beards along the way. I always carry my barber's tools with me. People who had been on the road for weeks and were in a hurry to get to the gold fields didn't have the time to look for a regular barber. They were mighty glad to find me at their camps of a night. I wasn't getting rich, but I was paying my own way.

Sitting on a log and sipping hot coffee, Charles Blessing would often watch as I wielded my scissors and exchanged small talk with the clients. One night, just before we reached Quesnel, a traveller paid overgenerously for his haircut. As the traveller left our campfire, newly trimmed, Blessing watched me tuck the coins into my money belt, and sighed.

He pulled out his own wallet, tipping the contents into his hand. I remember seeing two twenty-dollar gold pieces, and some smaller coins. Not a lot of money.

"I wish I had a trade the way you have, Moses," Blessing said to me. "I hadn't figured on this travelling being so expensive, and I'm running a bit short. I've only got about sixty dollars left and I need to buy a claim. It's twenty-five dollars for one hundred feet on Williams Creek, so I hear tell, and I have to get myself outfitted to work it, too. It's going to be close."

"You know you're always welcome to a bed at my shop in Barkerville, Charles," I said. "I've got an extra room in the back where I sleep. I can stake you, too, if you run out of grub. Once the ladies of the town see my new stock, the money will be coming in so fast I won't be able to count it!"

He looked at me, smiling. "That's a mighty kind offer, Moses, mighty kind. But before I'd ask another man to gamble on my prospecting or to feed me, I'd sell my luck."

"Your *luck*, Charles?"

"Yup. Right here. My nugget pin. It's California gold, and I figure if it brought me luck there it will bring me luck in the Cariboo." He carefully undid the pin and handed it to me. It was heavy, large, and curiously formed.

"Quite the nugget you have here, Charles."

"Look at it, Moses. Look at it carefully. Does the shape remind you of anything?"

I studied it hard. It did seem vaguely familiar, but I couldn't put my finger on what it reminded me of.

"Looks a bit like an angel spreading his wings," I said, hesitantly. "Not too much, but if you were to stretch your imagination that's what you could say it reminded you of."

"Right!" He was pleased, as if I were a school kid who'd guessed the right answer to a hard question. "Now, turn it around, Moses. Turn it upside-down."

Well, I turned the pin over and a man's face leapt out of the gold at me. "It's a face, a man's face, clear as a summer's day," I said. "Why, it's remarkable. I have never seen anything like that in a nugget before!"

"Right again!" Charles was smiling. "It does look like a face, but the jeweller who turned it into a stickpin for me didn't see it. He looked at it the other way around and only saw the angel. So he mounted the nugget upside down!

"Aren't too many people who ever get to see the face in it, though," he continued. "I keep it pretty close to me, even at night, and never take it off during the day. Wouldn't do to lose my luck now, would it? Before I've even got to Barkerville?" He carefully fastened the pin back on his lapel, making sure that it was secure. "Nope. Wouldn't do to lose my luck, wouldn't do at all!"

               *

Moses had finished his story. He looked at me, waiting for me to make the connection. I did.

"It was Charles Blessing's nugget that Mr. Barry was wearing, wasn't it Moses? It was Blessing's nugget, and Barry and Blessing left Quesnel together!"

"Yes, Ted. No one has seen my friend since the morning he left Quesnel with Barry, at least no one

I've been able to find. I'm worried. If Charles has lost his luck that means something pretty unfortunate has happened to him. And I suspect that James Barry knows more than he's telling.

"Are you sure, Moses, are you sure that it was the same nugget?"

"Theodore MacIntosh! Have you forgotten my story so quickly? The face in the gold could only be seen when the pin was turned upside down. As I trimmed Barry's hair I looked *down* at his lapel and saw it. The face in the nugget was there! There's no mistake, Ted, none. It's Charles Blessing's nugget that Barry has — Charles's luck."

5

A Dilemma

I stared at Moses, feeling my eyes grow wide. "That means ... that means that Mr. Barry must have stolen the nugget, doesn't it?"

"I'm sure he didn't come by it honestly, Ted. Look, if Charles Blessing had sold him the pin then Barry would have known about the face in it. It was such an unusual nugget and Charles was so proud of it that he surely would have shown the face to anyone who was buying it. And besides, Barry didn't have any money. He tried to borrow some from both me and Charles in Quesnel. How could he have bought the nugget?

"But Barry said it was his. He obviously didn't know how easy that particular nugget was to identify. Besides, Charles didn't need to sell it. He still had money left, almost the whole sixty dollars."

"Moses, if Barry has the pin and Barry was the last person known to be travelling with Mr. Blessing then ..."

"Don't say it, son. I've been thinking that way myself. I'm afraid that something very bad has happened to my friend — and I think that snake Barry was responsible!"

I stood up and started to leave the store. "Where do you think you're going?" called Moses.

"To fetch Constable Sullivan. You must tell him your suspicions, Moses. Mr. Blessing may be lying dead somewhere beside the road from Quesnel."

"Ted! Come back and sit down!" Moses's voice was sharp, almost angry. "Can't you see that I don't dare tell anyone, least of all an officer of the law, what I suspect? You heard what Barry said; something unfortunate would happen to you if word got out that I'd recognized the nugget. Barry's threatening to hurt you if I do talk, and knowing him he's liable to carry out that threat!"

"Huh! I'm not afraid of him!" I said, but deep inside I was hearing Barry's strange laugh and remembering how he had frightened me on the Richfield road. "He won't do anything to me," I repeated, but I guess my voice trembled a bit, because Moses smiled at me.

"Don't worry, Ted. You're safe as long as neither of us tells about the nugget."

I sat down on the bench again. "But Moses, Charles Blessing was a friend of yours. You can't keep quiet! We have to do something — James Barry may have murdered him!"

"We'll think on it, all right? If there were a way to keep you out of Barry's reach, then maybe I could tell the constable. But Barry's a sly one. You wouldn't be safe anywhere in Barkerville, not even in your own home."

"Maybe I could ..." I began.

"Don't worry about it for now, Ted. There's no way to keep you away from him. The way you wander the streets of this town, you'd be easy to find. Why, even your own mother doesn't know where you are half the time, does she? It could be hours before anyone even knew you were missing. Anything could happen. That man is one of the most evil people I have ever met!"

"I could stay right close to Pa until Barry's arrested," I suggested.

"You think he would be arrested? On what evidence? My word, and only mine, that he has my missing friend's stickpin? We need other proof before we can say anything!

"Besides, your pa isn't a much bigger man than I am, Ted. Do you really think he'd be any match for Barry?"

Moses was right. My pa is short and slender. Oh, he has strong enough arms from all the woodworking he does, but Barry is almost a foot taller. Much heavier, too. And meaner. I couldn't bear the thought of Pa getting tangled up with him on my account.

"I guess you're right, Moses. There isn't anything we can do." I took a deep breath. "I am afraid of Mr. Barry," I admitted. "He frightens me half to death, and I haven't even seen him really angry yet."

"I confess, he makes me nervous too," Moses said. He went to the cupboard and took out a small brown bottle.

"I'm not taking my courage from a bottle, Ted," he said, as he poured some of the thick liquid into a glass and added water. "Just sort of a precaution." He grimaced as he swallowed the mixture.

"Are you all right, Moses? Should I fetch the doctor?"

Moses laughed. "No, Ted. Sometimes when I'm upset, or perhaps a bit scared, my heart takes to racing some. Palpitations, they call it."

"Is it serious, Moses?" I asked, still worried about him.

"No, just a nuisance. This tonic fixes it up in a hurry, but it tastes so bad that I don't take it as often as I should."

He looked at his watch. "Wait with me, Ted. I have one more customer coming, then I'll close up early and walk you home. I don't like the idea of your being on that lonely road all by yourself today."

"Thanks, Moses. If you're sure you're all right?"

He nodded, and didn't say anything. Neither of us said anything, just sat there in silence. It was almost as if we were waiting for something to happen. We didn't know what, but both of us were sure it wouldn't be pleasant!

6

News!

It was late in the afternoon of September 27, 1866. I came running into the barbershop, a copy of the *Sentinel*, Barkerville's paper, clutched in my hand.

"Moses, Moses ..." I began.

"Ted, I have a customer right now." One of the saloon girls sat in the barber's chair, while Moses arranged her long hair in an elaborate nest of curls.

"But Moses, it's news, it's important!"

Moses frowned at me. His rule was that although I was allowed to stay in the shop while he had customers, I wasn't supposed to speak unless spoken to — just sit quietly and mind my own business. Moses didn't have many rules, and I'd never broken this one before.

"I'll speak to you later," he said.

Disappointed, I sat down and waited for him to finish with his hairstyling. The saloon girl spoke up. "Does the Sentinel have any news about the dead man found near Pinegrove? Oh, do read it aloud! I want to know more about it."

I looked at Moses. He had forgotten what he was

doing and stood, hands down at his sides, staring at me. His lips were pulled tightly together, and cords of muscle stood out on his neck.

"Yes, read it, Ted," he said at last.

I read. "Information was received on Tuesday evening, from the magistrate here, that the body of a man had been found in the woods ..." It went on to tell how a packer had discovered the body, but I skipped that part and jumped ahead. "The remains were in a very advanced stage of decomposition, the body being almost devoid of flesh and unrecognizable. The head rested on a coat, and the flesh of the lower side of the face still remained; a hole which is probably the effect of a bullet was observed in the skull, and from the position of the body it is evident that the man came to his death by foul means!"

"Oh, how awful!" burst out the saloon girl. "Do go on. I can hardly wait to hear the rest!"

Moses's hands were trembling as he arranged curls on the blond head. "Keep reading, Ted," he said softly.

I went on. "From the decomposed state of the body the deed must have been committed over a month ago. The body has not yet been identified, but it is more than probable that the clothes which still remain on it may lead to its identity."

There was silence in the room when I finished. "That's all," I said, "Except for a bit about sending someone to look at the body and having further particulars in another issue of the paper."

"Oh, my! That poor man. Decomposed like that! How terrible." The saloon girl tossed her head in agitation, much to the annoyance of Moses, who was still fussing with a curl. "Who do you suppose he was?" She went on. "Who on earth could he be?"

Still talking, anxious to spread the news to anyone who hadn't already heard it, she paid Moses. She gave him a larger than usual tip, and scurried out.

Moses sat down and put his head between his hands. "I think they've found my friend Charles!" His voice was low and muffled.

"It could be someone else, Moses. It could be."

"Pinegrove is only one day's travel from here, on the Quesnel road. It's about where Barry and Blessing would have stopped to camp for the night." He looked up suddenly. "I'm sure it's him, Ted. I feel it, somehow. I got a blackness of spirit when you read that news report, a blackness that is still hanging over me. I know it's Charles Blessing!"

I was quiet for a few minutes. Then ... "We have to tell Constable Sullivan now," I said. "We *have* to. Maybe you can identify Mr. Blessing's clothes, or some of his camp gear."

"But Barry ... and you ..." Moses didn't seem to be thinking too clearly. I felt sorry for him at that moment; he seemed to be suffering so. I went and put an arm around his shoulder.

"You must tell the constable, Moses. Otherwise you may never know if this dead man is Mr. Blessing or not. You're the only one who can identify him, if it is him. You're the only one in town who ever met him!"

He placed his hand over mine, pressing it firmly. "But what about you, Ted? We can't endanger you. What will we do to keep you safely away from James Barry?"

I thought for a minute. "I saw him going into Wake Up Jake's café just before I came here. He's probably still there. If you go right away to Constable Sullivan and tell him about Barry having the nugget and Mr. Blessing being missing for so long, I'm sure he'll arrest Barry. He'll keep him in jail, at least until the body is identified. Once he's in jail, I'll be safe."

"But until then?"

"Until Barry is in jail I'll ..." I stopped. I had no idea how I was going to keep safely out of the way until he was arrested. He might still be in the café where Constable Sullivan could find him easily. Or he might have left by now and be anywhere in Barkerville. He might even be looking for me!

Of course, we hadn't gone back on our promise. We hadn't said anything about Moses recognizing the nugget. But Barry would probably be thrown into a state of panic the moment he heard about the murdered man being found. He'd know that Moses could identify the body — if it were that of Charles Blessing. Moses also knew that Barry had been travelling with Mr. Blessing. So maybe Barry would carry out his threat, try to keep Moses quiet by doing something to me. I shuddered and looked around me.

"He's not here," said Moses, "and he won't be getting in if he comes here." He went to the door and put up the "Closed" sign, pulling the blinds over the windows and locking the door as he did.

He began to talk quickly, his voice stronger now. "You're right, Ted. I do have to report what I know to the constable. And the sooner the better."

"Can I come with you?" I asked, thinking I'd feel easier with big, burly Constable Sullivan beside me.

"No, I have a better idea. We'll leave by the back door, right now. I want you to run to your pa's shop, not stopping for anything, mind you. There are a lot of people on the street. You should be safe enough among them. Have your pa do the same as I did; put up the "Closed" sign, draw the blinds and bolt the door. Then the two of you stay there, not opening the door to anyone until you hear my voice.

"I'll go make my report to the constable. Then the moment I see Barry arrested, I'll come directly to you."

I nodded. It seemed like the best plan. Pa's shop had only one door and it could be secured on the inside with a strong bolt.

"Now remember, go directly to your pa's. And once that door is locked, don't open it for anyone except me. Tell your pa what's happened, the whole story. You might also suggest that he keep one of his biggest hammers close by, just in case."

Quietly we crept out the back door. "Run, Ted, run," whispered Moses, and I set off, running as I'd never run before.

It wasn't far to Pa's carpentry shop, but I planned to go down the back street until I was nearly there, then cut between two buildings to get to the main street. I wanted to stay off the main street for as long as possible. That was where Wake Up Jake's was — and maybe James Barry.

I was nearly there. Still running, I tore around the corner of the building behind Pa's shop, ducked into the narrow passageway that led to the main street and ran right into a tall man.

My head must have hit him at about chest level, for I heard the air leave his lungs with a rush. "Hey!" he shouted, grabbing my shoulders and shaking me, "Watch where you're going, you little ..."

It was James Barry.

7

Captured!

I panicked as I saw the glint of recognition in Barry's eyes. "Well, if it isn't Master Percy," he said, tightening his grip on me. "This *is* a pleasant surprise. And just where do you think you're off to in such a hurry?"

"Let me go, you murderer! Let me go! They know all about you!"

He held me more firmly. "*Murderer*, is it now? There hasn't been a body found, Master Percy. How can there be a murder without a body?"

He hadn't heard about the body being discovered! So he hadn't been looking for me; I had just run into him by accident. Well, then, perhaps he could be persuaded to let me go. I tried.

"I'm sorry, Mister Barry. I didn't mean to bump into you. You startled me, that's all. I don't know anything about any murder, sir, and that's the truth."

He looked at me hard before he spoke. "I don't believe you, young Percy. I think you know something you're not telling me."

I looked around desperately, hoping that someone

would come into the narrow passageway, someone who could help me. We were still alone. I avoided Barry's menacing eyes as I answered, "I don't know anything, sir. Please, let me go now. My pa is waiting for me."

"He'll have to wait a little longer, then. You and I need to have a talk."

Still holding me firmly with one hand, he reached under his jacket with the other and drew out a gun. "See this, Master Percy? She's my constant companion. Never leaves my side. Always loaded, too. Now, I want you to walk on ahead of me, not too far ahead, mind, right out onto the main street. Keep going, up towards the trail to Richfield, just as if you were going towards home. Me and my friend here will be right behind you, real close. Anyone talks to you, you answer polite and nice like, then just keep walking, understand?"

He released my arm and slipped the gun into his pocket. "Move on now, Master Percy. Do as I told you or your mother'll be a-weeping over your body before the day is much older."

I guess I'm a coward. I did exactly what he told me to do.

We came out of the passageway between the buildings, onto the main street, and turned towards Richfield. Barry stayed a few steps behind me all the way. I turned back to look at him once. He put his hand into his pocket, the one that held the gun. My legs were quivering but I kept going.

Thankfully, no one spoke to me. I don't think I could have answered in anything like a normal voice. I didn't try to run. I just kept walking slowly, knowing all the time that he was right behind me, waiting for me to make a mistake.

We reached the end of Barkerville's main street, and began the long climb to Richfield. The road was empty, probably because it was near dinner time. As we passed my house I looked at it hopefully, willing Ma or Pa to appear at the door and call me in. But, although I could see Ma moving around in the lighted dining room, she didn't see me in the dusk outside. I guess Barry didn't know exactly where on the Richfield road I lived, or he would have made us detour around my house. I didn't look back as we passed the house but kept going, climbing upwards.

A few hundred yards farther on, Barry turned off the road. "This way, Master Percy," he called, bringing the gun out of his pocket and gesturing with it. "This way."

A narrow, overgrown path led up the hillside. There was a cabin ahead, deserted by the looks of it. The door sagged ajar and several of the windows were broken. It must have belonged to a miner who had worked out his claim and left Barkerville; there were many such places on this road.

We went into the cabin where it was dark, very dark. Barry motioned me to stand against a wall. He produced the stub of a candle from somewhere and lit it. Dark, eerie shadows crept along the walls. I shuddered.

He pointed to a rough wooden bench against one wall. "Sit down and start talking! Explain why you called me a murderer just now. Has that fool Moses been talking out of turn?"

"No, sir." I could hardly speak, my mouth was so dry. "No sir. Moses hasn't said anything to me — or to anyone," I added hastily. "You just frightened me when I ran into you like that, sir. I didn't mean what I said."

"Huh! That's not good enough you little trouble-maker!"

He lifted the gun and it made a small click as he pointed it at me. I jumped, and he laughed. "She's ready to shoot now," he said. "Talk!"

I swallowed hard. I squirmed on the bench and looked frantically around for help, for something, anything. Barry stared at me, waiting. He held the gun level with my head. "Talk!" he said again. "Quickly, now. I'm losing my patience."

My face felt hot and flushed with shame, but I talked. I told him everything — that Moses had recognized the nugget, that the body had been discovered, and that Moses had already gone to tell Constable Sullivan what he suspected.

Barry cursed. "That interfering little wart! Why couldn't he mind his own business?"

Somewhere within me I found the courage to speak. "So you see, they already know. You might as well let me go, because if I'm missing they'll know you have me ..."

He just stared at me. "And who is to tell them where you are?" he said, sneering. "Who is going to come to your rescue, young Percy, if I don't let you go?"

I didn't answer. I couldn't.

He walked to the broken window and rested his elbows on the dusty sill, looking out into the night. He seemed to have forgotten about me. Maybe I could make a run for the open door? I moved slightly on the bench, tensing my leg muscles for a dash to freedom.

He must have caught the motion out of a corner of his eye, for he suddenly whirled around to face me.

"Don't try it," he snapped. "I'm a good shot. You'd be dead before you reached the door."

For a while there was silence as he thought. Then he spoke. "Thanks to you and that meddling Moses, I have to get out of town in a hurry. Now that I know the police will be looking for me, I'll have to stick to the woods and the creek bank and stay off the main road, out of sight." He picked up a loaded pack sack from one corner of the room. "Luckily enough I prepared for this unfortunate turn of events. I'm ready to move on."

"They'll catch you. They'll catch you for sure."

"Just let them try. They'll never find me. I've got a friend, a good friend, not too many days travel from here. He'll look after me and see me safely out of the country. A few miles after I swing across the bridge, I'm safe!"

His mouth twisted into an ugly smile. "But I can't have you running around telling them that I've left town, now can I? If the constables don't know that I've gone, then they'll spend hours searching Barkerville and Rich-field looking for me. I need them off on that wild goose chase while I make tracks out of here."

He was still smiling. I didn't like it.

"I'll have to take care of you, won't I, Master Percy?"

It almost seemed as if my heart stopped when I realized what he had said. Take *care* of me? Did that mean he was going to ...?

He knew what I was thinking. "Say your prayers, Percy, and be quick about it!" He moved closer, bringing the gun to rest against the side of my head. "Say your prayers," he repeated.

8

The Clue

I heard the creek before I opened my eyes, and for a moment I thought I was home, in my own bed. Then I became aware that I was lying on something hard. My feet were cold and my shoulders ached. I tried to stretch, to ease the soreness, and suddenly my eyes flew open and I was wide awake! I was lying on the floor of the abandoned miner's cabin where James Barry had left me, trussed up like a sack of potatoes!

My first thought was, *I'm alive!* I shivered as I remembered Barry pointing his gun at my head. I must have fainted, but what I couldn't understand was why I was still alive. He had certainly meant to kill me. Perhaps, when I fainted, he changed his mind, decided that he didn't want two murders on his conscience.

The candle had long since gone out, and the only light in the cabin was moonlight that came through the open door. The corners of the room were dark, very dark. I wondered if Barry were still there, in the shack, waiting for me to wake up. "Hello?" I called out, "Is anybody there?" It wasn't the smartest thing to say, but it was all I could think of.

I waited a while, but no one answered. No tall, dark shape detached itself from the shadowy corners and came out, laughing. Barry was gone.

I wriggled my shoulders, and managed to sit up. James Barry may have gone, but I was still here, and in a most awkward situation. What was I to do?

Throughout the long night the shadows deepened, taking over more of the cabin as the moon moved behind the hill. I tried everything I could think of to get free.

I shouted, yelled, even screamed for help. No one came. I struggled to my feet, hog-tied though I was, and tried to make my way out of the cabin. The ropes around my ankles were tight, my feet were numb, and I fell flat on my face three times in a row. I pulled against the ropes that tied me, trying desperately to loosen them. They remained firm and secure. I even cried a bit as I realized how cold, hungry, thirsty, and utterly miserable I was. That only made things worse as my nose began to run, and I couldn't get my hands free to tend to it.

Finally I did the only thing I could. I inched my way to a wall, settled myself against it as comfortably as I could, and waited for someone to find me.

It was a long night, the longest I've ever spent. I couldn't sleep; I was too uncomfortable. I couldn't ease the pressure on my shoulders, and they hurt dreadfully. My feet finally stopped aching, going completely numb. Then I began to worry about frostbite. September nights can be cold in this mountain country and tonight was no exception.

I listened to the creek talking to itself, to an owl calling to its mate, to the strange little rustling sounds the mice made as they scurried about the cabin floor. Something ran over my legs once, and I jumped. I waited, watching the dark patch behind the open door gradually lighten as dawn approached. Then, just when the sun began to win its battle with the night, I fell asleep.

I woke, how much later I don't know, to broad daylight and the sound of voices outside the cabin. "Here!" I called my voice weak and dry, "Here! I'm in here!"

Moses and Constable Sullivan burst through the doorway. Moses looked dreadful, as if he, too, had been awake all night. "Ted, Ted, are you all right?"

I nodded my head and managed to croak, "Water, please," as Constable Sullivan began to untie me.

When he finished, the constable produced a small flask. "I've water right here, Ted."

Moses knelt beside me. "We've been looking for you all night, Ted. Are you sure you aren't hurt?"

I tried to stand but I couldn't. The ropes had been too tight and my legs had lost all feeling. Moses pulled off my boots and sat beside me, rubbing my feet. As the circulation began to return they started tingling, then hurting.

"I'm sorry, Ted," he said. "I know it's painful. But we have to get the blood moving again. Just grit your teeth and try to bear it. The hurt won't last long."

As Moses worked on my feet, Constable Sullivan told me what had happened. He had heard Moses's story and had begun the search for Barry when Moses came rushing back to say that I had never reached the safety of my pa's carpentry shop. The news of my disappearance spread rapidly, and almost the whole town had turned out to search — but for me, not for James Barry. Pa and some other men were up at Richfield, working their way down, checking every house, empty or not. Moses and the constable had started from the Barkerville end of the road, doing the same thing. A group of miners was wading up the creek, making sure my *body* hadn't been thrown there.

"We didn't expect to find you alive, Ted," said the constable. "But thank God you're all right. Your poor ma has been hysterical with worry. Now, tell us what happened."

I told them. I hung my head when I came to the part about my telling James Barry everything he had wanted to know. "I'm sorry, sir, but he had a gun and I was frightened. So I told him that the body had been found and that we suspected it was Mr. Blessing's."

"No need to be sorry, Ted. I would have done the same thing myself. No point in getting hurt over a piece of news that he was bound to hear sooner or later anyway."

"Thank you, Constable. But I also told him that Moses had recognized the nugget. I shouldn't have done that."

"Don't you worry your head about that, son. He probably suspected it, anyway.

"Now, the important thing is, did he say anything about where he was heading? We want to catch that man. We're *going* to catch him." His face hardened as he spoke, his eyes narrowing, and for a minute I almost felt sorry for Barry. I'd hate to have Constable Sullivan after me!

"He said he had a friend — a friend who would help him get out of the country."

"Did he indeed, now?" The constable stood straighter and his face grew solemn. Moses stopped rubbing my feet and stayed still, listening. "And who might that friend be, do you think?"

"I'm sorry, Constable. He didn't say a name. He was going to tell me where he was heading, but he caught himself in time and didn't finish the sentence. I'm afraid I don't know anything that can help."

"Think, Ted, think!" Constable Sullivan insisted. "He's got a good fifteen hours start on us now. We have to catch up to him. Didn't he give you any clue as to where he was going?"

"No, nothing." I felt terrible. Because they'd spent all night looking for me, James Barry had managed to get out of town without being caught. "He didn't say anything else."

I paused. "Well, he did mention that once he got across the bridge he was safe. But he didn't say which bridge."

The constable's face seemed even redder, and his words came out in a rush. "His words, Ted, his exact words. Can you remember them?"

I thought hard. It seemed so long ago. What I remembered most clearly was Barry smiling and saying he'd have to take care of me. "I don't know," I said. "It's been such a long night. I've forgotten."

"Think, son, think! It's of great importance."

I thought. They watched my face intently, almost as if they were trying to help me remember. "Well," I said at last, "I think what he said was, 'Once I swing across the bridge ...' No, it was, 'A few miles after I swing across the bridge, I'm safe.' I'm pretty sure those were his exact words."

The constable frowned. "Swing across a bridge, eh? I wonder." He was silent for a long time. Moses helped me get up. I could stand now and walk, too, if I went slowly. My feet still tingled, but they didn't hurt anymore.

"Please, can I go home?" I asked. I was suddenly near tears and fought to keep them back. "I'm tired and hungry, and I want to see my ma and pa because they've been so worried. Can we go?"

"Of course, Ted," said Moses. "Here, lean on me and I'll help you. It's not far to your house, and your ma has hot soup and biscuits ready. I told her you'd be hungry when we found you."

"Wait a minute!" Constable Sullivan's face was so red that it almost glowed, and his eyes sparkled like sunlight on the creek. "Are you sure that's what he said? About swinging across a bridge?"

"I think so. Yes, I'm positive."

"Then I do know where he's going! There's only one suspension bridge on the Cariboo Road — at Alexandra, just north of Yale. I'll take even money that the bridge at Alexandra is where he's heading. He was thinking of that bridge and how it sways in the wind. That's why he used the word 'swing.' All we have to do is stop him there, before he crosses the bridge and reaches this friend who will look after him!"

"Do you think so?" I asked, my tiredness and hunger almost forgotten. "Do you really think so?"

"I'm sure of it," replied the constable. "Positive. Judging by what he said, it's the only place he could be going. I'll take the stage tomorrow, and with any luck, I should intercept him before he's across that bridge. He'll be walking, I reckon, sticking to the side of the road and trying to stay out of sight. Even if he could manage to get a ride somewhere, he wouldn't have tried to do it yet, not this close to Barkerville. I'll be at the bridge before him for sure. We've nearly got him. Yes, we've nearly got him!"

His face suddenly fell and his voice lost its high, excited note. "Only trouble is, I've never seen James Barry. I wouldn't recognize him no matter where I found him."

"We can tell you what he looks like," I said. "He's dark and tall and has a beard and ..."

"Ted, do you have any idea how many tall, dark, bearded men there are in this part of the world? I'm liable to come back with the wrong man!"

There was silence in the cabin, a silence so deep that the sound of Williams Creek suddenly seemed loud. Then Moses spoke, softly, his voice hardly disturbing the quiet.

"I'll go with you, Constable. I would consider it an honour to assist you in apprehending the killer of my friend, Charles Blessing. I wasn't much help to Charles in life; kind of blame myself for not going on to Barkerville with him instead of staying behind in Quesnel for that extra day. Maybe now I can be of help to him. I'll come with you. I'll point James Barry out to you. You won't return with the wrong man."

Constable Sullivan coughed, and the stillness was broken. "Appreciate your help, Moses. You'll be more than welcome to come with me. Between the two of us we'll make sure that Barry comes back to Barkerville and gets his just rewards for the evil he's done."

I stared at Moses, unable to speak. I knew I'd never dare point Barry out to the law, be the one responsible for his arrest. But they'd be bringing him back here, back to Barkerville! The last thing I wanted was to see James Barry ever again.

Deep inside of me a tiny, cowardly voice spoke, and I heard it, even though I didn't want to. "I hope you're long gone, Mr. Barry," the shameful little voice said, "I hope they don't catch you and bring you back here. I hope I never see you again, even if that means you escape from the law."

9

Murderer on the Loose!

C onstable Sullivan was eager to get away as soon as possible to try to catch up with Barry, but Chief Constable Fitzgerald had other ideas.

"Listen, Sullivan," he told him, "We don't even know for sure that the dead man is Charles Blessing. He may have been someone different."

Constable Sullivan protested, "But then why would Barry be in such a hurry to get out of town? And why would he have bothered to tie up Ted that night so he could get a head start?"

"I'm not saying it isn't Blessing's body, now, or that Barry isn't a murderer," the chief constable went on, "Only that we have to do things properly. The inquest is set for October 1. If Moses can identify the body and the coroner says it is Charles Blessing, then you can set out the next day. If Barry is heading for the suspension bridge he'll be travelling by foot, and probably only at night. You take the stage and you'll be there days before him — lots of time to set a trap. Just hold your horses, Sullivan, and wait for the inquest. We're sworn members of the police force, and we have to do things official-like."

At the inquest, Moses did identify the body as that of his friend Charles Blessing. He didn't have to actually look at the corpse. I guess nobody wanted to look at it. It had been lying out in the open for nearly four months and must have been a terrible sight. Poor Mr. Blessing was buried in a hurry, right close to where he had been found with the bullet hole in his head.

Moses recognized three items — a new tin drinking cup, a sheath knife, and a silver pencil case — all found either on or near the body, and all three bearing the initials C.M.B. "Charles bought that tin cup in Quesnel," he told the coroner. "His own had fallen off his pack earlier on the road, and he needed a new one. I was with him when he bought it, and saw him scratch his initials on the bottom."

Of Charles Blessing's money, the almost $60.00 he had with him shortly before his murder, and the gold nugget stickpin which Moses said he always wore, there was, of course, no trace. Moses would have more testifying to do if James Barry ever came to trial!

Moses took up a collection from his friends and customers, and hired my pa to carve a headstone and build a picket fence around Mr. Blessing's grave at Pinegrove. The money poured in, almost as if everyone in Barkerville felt ashamed that a murderer had walked their streets, and they wanted to make amends to the dead man. The collection grew to $94.50, a handsome amount. The headstone would read, "In memory of C.M. Blessing, a native of Ohio, Aged 30 years. Was murdered near this spot, May 31st, 1866." Moses thought his friend was from Ohio, he seemed to remember him mentioning it, but he had to guess about his age.

Meanwhile, in the days between the discovery of the body and the inquest, more excitement gripped the town. Travellers coming into the gold fields reported seeing a tall, heavily bearded man on the road. His behaviour puzzled them, for he avoided all company, hid beside the road whenever a stage passed, and travelled mainly in the dark. Stumbling into camps at night he had been offered the hospitality of the road; a chance to sit, drink a mug of coffee, and pass on news of the Creek. He curtly refused all offers and quickly left, keeping his face well out of the light of the campfires. The travellers were puzzled. Here was a man leaving the gold fields when almost everyone else was going to them. His strange behaviour and sullen manner intrigued them, and they spread their stories eagerly in Barkerville.

That afternoon, right after the inquest had finished, Moses was shaving one such traveller, and listening to his story. Moses's business had almost doubled since Blessing's body had been found, and he had told his story of the strangely shaped gold nugget. Customers came to get their hair done, their beards trimmed, to buy his select stock of items for the ladies — and also to listen to whatever he could tell them, first-hand, about his friendship with the murdered man. There had never been a murder in Barkerville and the whole town could talk of nothing else.

The newcomer in the barber's chair had finished his tale, "I'm sure it was this Barry that I saw," he said as he left the shop. "Thank the stars he didn't accept my hospitality and spend the night by my fire. Why, I might have been murdered myself!" He hurried out, eyes wide with the thought of his narrow escape.

There were still two customers waiting, when a third came in the door. Moses smiled at the newcomer and said, "Be a few minutes before I can tend to you, sir. Hope you don't mind waiting." As he readied the chair for the next customer he sighed and rubbed his hand across his eyes, but by the time he began the haircut his voice was firm and there was a smile on his lips again.

I waved goodbye, and left the barbershop. It was good for Moses to have his business increase so much, but he was too busy to spend any time talking with me. To be honest though, I was sick to death of hearing the story of the gold nugget stickpin and the death of Charles Blessing. Actually, I admitted to myself as I walked slowly up to Pa's shop, it wasn't the nugget stickpin or Mr. Blessing I was tired of hearing about, it was James Barry. His name was on everyone's lips these days, especially in Moses's shop where it seemed that his name was mentioned every minute. I didn't want to hear any more of Mr. James Barry than I had to. I had seen quite enough of him already, and I just wanted to forget all about him, and as soon as possible.

Pa was gluing a rocking chair together when I got there, and I took over stirring the pot of thick, strong-smelling glue on the stove where Pa was heating it. "Won't be too long, Ted, then we'll walk home together, if you feel like the company." I nodded without speaking. Lately I preferred to walk home with Pa, rather than go by myself. We didn't say much on the way, but I felt better with him by my side, even though I knew that James Barry was miles away from Barkerville, making his slow way towards the Alexandra Bridge where he hoped to find help and safety.

Pa had finished with the glue, and was tightening the clamps around the chair's joints, ready to leave his work for the night, when someone knocked on the shop door, then pushed it open and came in.

"Constable Sullivan," said Pa. "All ready for your trip? I hear you and Moses are going out on tomorrow's stage, off to arrest James Barry."

The constable's face was serious as he pulled off his cap, and stood awkwardly twisting it around in his hands.

"There's been a wee problem with that, Mr. MacIntosh," he said, and his eyes turned towards me. "That's why I'm here. I need your help. Or rather, I need Ted's help."

I shoved the brush back into the hot glue, and felt my face go red. "Me?" I said, and my voice sounded high and thin, "What can I ..."

"It's Moses, Ted. He can't go with me to point out James Barry."

"But ..." I said, "I just left his shop, not an hour ago, and he was telling everyone how he would be on that stage tomorrow, how he would bring Mr. Barry back to face justice for murdering his friend, Mr. Blessing."

"I know, Ted, but Moses isn't a young man anymore. He's fifty, and he's got this little heart problem."

I nodded. "Pal — pal — something or other. Yes, he takes a tonic for it sometimes."

"It must have been the worry about going with me that brought it on, the worry and all the extra work he's had since this murder. He got pretty sick just after you left his shop, Ted. The doctor is with him now."

"Moses!" I half turned, ready to go to the barbershop.

"He's all right, Ted, really. He'll be fine in a few days, Doc Wilkinson promised. He just needs to rest, stay right in bed, and take that tonic regular like."

"A few days? But he can't stay in bed now! You've got to get down to the bridge and try to stop Barry. Moses can't be sick now!"

Pa looked at me strangely, and there was an edge in his voice when he spoke. "Ted! A man cannot choose the time of his illnesses, as you well know. I should think your concern should be for Mr. Moses's health, not for his ability to catch that murderer."

I swallowed. I hadn't meant to sound uncaring. I *did* care about Moses, and I *did* want him to be well. But — but if Moses couldn't go with the constable to identify James Barry, then how would he know the right man to arrest? The constable had never seen James Barry.

But I had. I would recognize James Barry anywhere. And I knew, knew before he ever spoke, why Constable Sullivan was here, in Pa's shop.

"No!" I said, not waiting to hear the words from the constable himself, "No. I can't do it. I won't go with you, Constable. Please, please don't ask me to."

Pa and Constable Sullivan looked at each other. Then they both turned and stared at me. I went back to stirring the glue in the pot, stirring it so hard that some of it splashed over the edge onto the hot stove, sending up thick clouds of foul-smelling smoke. The burning glue must have stung my eyes, because they began to water, and I turned away and brushed at them with my sleeve.

"That is what you want, isn't it Constable?" asked Pa. "You need someone who can identify James Barry to go with you tomorrow, and you want Ted here to accompany you?"

"Yes, sir. There's no one else in town who knows the man well enough to make a positive identification. I need Master Ted, sir, with your permission of course. He'll be well looked after, and there'll be no danger to him. I'll see to that."

"Ted? Well, Ted? It seems to me that you are being called to do your duty as a law-abiding citizen. You have my permission, and I'm sure your mother's, to go with Constable Sullivan if you wish. It would make us both proud to know that our son is helping the law."

I stirred at the glue again, not looking up, not meeting their eyes. I didn't want to go. I didn't want to have to point out James Barry to the law. I didn't want to have to see him ever again. But Moses would want me to go; he wanted James Barry caught. And my pa, I knew he would be disappointed in me if I weren't brave enough to go. Oh, he wouldn't say much, and he wouldn't punish me, but he'd be disappointed, and I'd know it and see it in his eyes every time he looked at me.

Still without looking up I said, "I'll go, then. I'll be on that stagecoach with you tomorrow, Constable."

Moses was my friend. I wanted to help him and I wanted Pa to be proud of me, and so I would go. But that didn't mean I was in any way looking forward to the journey. I was scared already, and I hadn't even left Barkerville.

10

The Journey

I t seemed as if the whole town had gathered in front of Barnard's Express office the next morning to see us off. Ma and Pa, proud that I had made the decision to go with the constable, smiled at me and warned me to mind my manners. A few saloon girls threw me kisses (well, perhaps it was actually Constable Sullivan they were aiming at) and a crowd of miners gathered around to shake our hands and wish us luck. Moses was there, too, walking slowly over to the stagecoach, leaning on a cane and looking tired.

"Moses! You're supposed to be in bed. The doctor said you need to rest."

"I'll have rest enough once I see you safely on your way, Ted. But I had to come and wish you God speed. And — and thank you, Ted." He took my hand in his and pressed firmly. "My thoughts will be with you."

"Don't you worry, Mr. Moses," said Constable Sullivan. "We'll bring Mr. Barry back here to face justice, you'll see. Just get yourself well again."

"I shall, Constable, knowing that the boy is in good hands, and that the murderer of my friend will be caught soon. May God go with the both of you." He slowly made his way back to the barbershop. I could see him as he sat down at the table by the window, and began to write in a large book. Moses's famous diary! At last I had found a place in it. How would the entry read, I wondered. Perhaps something like, "On this day the second of October, 1866, Master Theodore MacIntosh and Constable Sullivan departed on the stage for Alexandra for the purpose of apprehending one James Barry, a most probable murderer."

Barry. I shouldn't have thought of him. Although I was showing a good front as the stage pulled out and the crowd waved and cheered, I was very frightened inside. I didn't want to be going. I didn't want to be responsible for the arrest of that man.

I forced myself to stop thinking about it. There was nothing I could do. I'd made a promise to Moses, and now I had to see it through. I settled back and tried to enjoy the trip.

The journey took about four days, fifty-two hours of actual travelling time. It was a demanding schedule for horses and passengers alike. The horses were changed every eighteen or twenty miles, and the passengers rested and ate about every six hours. We'd stop for the night at a roadhouse around seven or eight in the evening — later, if we ran into delays. We'd eat and tumble wearily into bed after our day of being bounced around on the road. Departure time was four the next morning, much too early for my liking. By the third day on the road I was exhausted, and regretting that I'd ever agreed to come.

"Chin up, Master Ted." Constable Sullivan didn't seem any the worse for the long journey. His round face was as cheerful as ever, and he didn't look at all tired. "Only one more day of travel, then you can rest."

I looked out the stagecoach window, trying not to let him know how miserable I was feeling.

"How fast do you suppose we're going right now?" I asked, more to take my mind off my troubles than because I was really interested.

"I reckon about five or so miles an hour, maybe a bit more," replied the constable. "We'll ask the driver if you like."

He stuck his head out the window and hollered to our driver. "Hey, Mr. Tingley, what's our estimated speed in this rig?"

Stephen Tingley was our driver's name, a name that lent itself to many crude jokes about how the seat of his pants must feel after all the years he had bounced around on a stagecoach. He carried a long whip, but he seldom used it on the horses. Stagecoach drivers were trained thoroughly for their jobs, and seemed to have a special relationship with the animals they guided. The horses, too, were unusual. We entered and left all settlements at a fast gallop, the horses tossing their heads as if they were showing off to the lazy town animals. Sometimes, on a steep curve, they seemed to know when to hold back or when to put on an extra burst of speed all by themselves, without any help from the driver.

"Who wants to know?" Mr. Tingley shouted back in answer to the constable's question.

"Master Ted is curious. Wants to know how soon he can apprehend his murderer!" the constable yelled.

"Tell Master Ted that we're going a steady six miles an hour, and he'll be at the bridge tomorrow evening. He's welcome to come and join me on the driver's box after the next change of horses. I reckon he's getting pretty bored with all you dull passengers back there!"

The constable grinned at me. "Did you hear that?" he asked. "Dull people, are we? Well, we'll show Mr. Tingley on the return trip when we have a murderer to keep us company!"

I enjoyed riding up front, watching the horses, their muscles bunching and relaxing as they ran, and being able to see ahead to the next curve. Also, Mr. Tingley had a pocket full of licorice (his only vice he told me) and he shared generously. He was very kind to me, even allowing me to hold the reins on the straight stretches. He seemed to sense how much I was dreading the coming encounter, how afraid I was of James Barry. Although he never did say anything directly about our mission, he managed to make me feel more comfortable about it.

"It's a fine thing to help the law men in their sworn duty," he said once. Then again, "If I make the return trip before you're ready to leave, I'll make sure I see your ma and tell her you arrived safely." I hadn't said anything about being homesick, but I confess I was, a bit. I had never been away from home by myself before, and the long trip, early hours and strange beds had left me feeling a little sorry for myself.

The next evening when we stopped at the suspension bridge at Alexandra, just a few miles north of Yale, not even Mr. Tingley's cheery parting words could raise my spirits. The red and yellow coach, the colours a trademark of all Barnard's equipment, pulled away from the bridge, the passengers leaning out the windows and shouting words of luck and advice. The stage rattled around a curve in the road, Mr. Tingley raised his whip in farewell, and then the coach was gone.

"Well, Ted, this is it. We'll go into the tollhouse now, and wait for Mr. James Barry to put in an appearance. I hope we haven't missed him."

I didn't have the heart to say so to the constable, but I hoped that James Barry was long gone and far away by now — that we *had* missed him. Murderer or not, I didn't want to have to see him ever again in my life!

11

At the Bridge

The Alexandra suspension bridge is one of the world's modern wonders. It was built only three years ago, in 1863, and there isn't another bridge like it anywhere in the West.

It is 300 feet long and hangs across the Fraser River on thick cables attached to strong supports. At the end there is a large gate, stretching right across the width of the bridge, and a small house where the tollkeeper lives. He is responsible for collecting the money for passage from stages, freight wagons, and foot passengers alike. Although you can cross the bridge from the one end, you can't set foot on the other side until you pay your money and the tollkeeper unlocks the gate. Coming the other way, you have to pay before you get more than a few steps onto the bridge. No one can get across the river without being seen. This bridge was the perfect place to set a trap for James Barry.

The tollkeeper, an old man who shuffled when he walked, took us into the small house after locking the gate, which had a large bell attached to it. Travellers at night would ring the bell until the noise woke the tollkeeper, and he came to take their money, and let them pass.

I was shown to a bed in one corner of the room. It was small and covered with blankets that didn't look very clean, but I fell down on it thankfully, I was too tired to even want to eat. Just before dozing off, I heard Constable Sullivan and the tollkeeper making plans.

Having made sure that no one of Barry's description had crossed the river in the last few days, the constable seemed to relax. "Well, then he's still behind us on the road. We'll get him for sure." Carefully he placed his gun and handcuffs on the table.

He explained how Barry would almost certainly be travelling at night, and alone. The constable and I were to stay hidden in the gatehouse at all times. Once the bell rang, announcing the arrival of a traveller, I was to peer through a small window, one that afforded a good view of anyone waiting by the gate. The tollkeeper was to meet the traveller as he usually did, but would hold his lantern so that the light fell on the stranger's face. If it were Barry, I would signal to the constable who would slip out the back door and be waiting, handcuffs and gun ready to seize Barry the moment he set foot on the road by the bridge. I heard the tollkeeper tell Constable Sullivan that he could lie in wait for Barry behind the large tree just at the edge of the bridge. I must have fallen asleep after they left to check the hiding place because I never did hear them come back into the house.

I was awakened once that night. The constable's voice was gentle as he shook me, and I could hear the muffled clanging of the bell, announcing the arrival of a late traveller. "Come, lad. We've work to do."

I rubbed my eyes fiercely as I took up my post by the small window, listening to the old keeper's voice. "I'm coming, I'm coming. Just hold your horses for a while," he shouted. A shadowy figure stood by the gate, impatiently pulling the rope that rang the bell. The tollkeeper angled the light from his lantern to fall on the stranger's face. "Just a moment, now. Let's have a look at you, see who is waking me from my hard-earned rest."

A short, blond young man was revealed in the flickering lantern light. I sighed. "It's not Barry," I said. "It's not anything like him." The stranger passed through the gate and went on his way, unaware of the trap he had just gone through. We found our way back to our beds.

The rest of the night passed without further excitement. So did the next day. By that evening I was bored. Having to stay out of sight meant that I was confined to the small gatehouse. I could listen to the rattle of coaches on the bridge, hear the voices of foot travellers, but I had to stay away from the window. I couldn't see anyone or anything. The constable wasn't taking any chances of my being seen. "Just in case Barry decides to have a little look-see during the day, before he tries to cross the bridge," he explained. "If he catches a glimpse of you, or me either, he'll turn tail and run like a scared rabbit. We have to make him believe that it's safe to cross, that we haven't caught up with him yet."

We sat in the gloomy house throughout the long day, waiting for the dark which might bring James Barry within our reach. With a strange feeling of uneasiness, I watched the night fall. We didn't know for sure that tonight would be the night Barry would try to cross the river. Constable Sullivan said that it might be as long as a week yet, depending on how fast Barry travelled and how often he stopped to rest or hide. But James Barry was coming, coming to meet his destiny, as surely as the stars come out in a clear night sky. I was a large part of that destiny — and I didn't want to be!

It was sometime after midnight when once again I was shaken awake. The tollkeeper was pulling on his boots, muttering to himself about being awakened two nights in a row. The bell sounded clearly, ringing urgently in the dark.

I took up my post at the window, my heart pounding. Again the tollkeeper made his slow way to the gate, again he lifted the lantern so that I could see the traveller's face. This time it was a tall man, dark, but not bearded. He sported a luxurious moustache, the ends curling upwards and carefully waxed to keep them in place. I remember thinking that a moustache like that would be hard to keep tidy while travelling, and wondering why he bothered with it. I studied him closely as the tollkeeper fumbled with the lock, giving me lots of time to make the identification. "No," I said, finally. "It's not him." I turned, relieved, and started back towards my bed.

I could hear footsteps as the stranger and the tollkeeper passed the house together. "I'm sorry to awaken you, old man, but my business is urgent. Here, take this for your trouble."

He must have come across with a good tip, for the tollkeeper replied, "I'd waken every night, and gladly, for such compensation."

"And I would gladly pay it every night, for my freedom." Then the stranger laughed.

I whirled around. There was no mistaking that laugh. The sound of it made shivers run up and down my spine, and my heart began to beat at twice its normal rate.

"Constable ..." I began.

"What is it, Ted?" You look as if you've seen a ghost."

"Quickly, Constable, quickly! It's him, it's James Barry!"

The words had hardly left my mouth when the constable was gone, slipping out of the house as silently as a shadow. I sat down at the table, my head between my hands, waiting. Would he be in time? Would he be able to spring his trap, to capture Barry as he stepped off the bridge? Or would he be too late, and would a man who was probably a murderer have reached freedom?

It would be my fault if Barry escaped, if he managed to make a dash for freedom. I had not recognized him soon enough, not given Constable Sullivan enough time to reach his hiding place and be ready to take Barry by surprise. It would be my fault if he got away. I had stared too hard at the stranger's moustache, and forgotten to look at his eyes. I had let the constable down, let Moses down.

"Oh, catch him, Constable," I half prayed under my breath. Then, without being able to help myself, the next words slipped out. "Oh, don't catch him, Constable! Don't bring him back here for me to face!"

12

We Return

The tollkeeper didn't have to ask any questions when he came back to the house. One look at my face told him the whole story. "Ha! That *was* your Mr. Barry, then." He looked thoughtfully at the coin in his hand, then shrugged and pocketed it, "Oh, well. I guess his money's no different from any other man's."

There were footsteps outside and both of us looked up. The door flew open and James Barry, his hands cuffed behind him, stumbled through the doorway. Right behind him came Constable Sullivan, his gun drawn. The trap had been sprung!

I shrank back against my chair. Now that I saw Barry close up I recognized the hard, glittering eyes and wondered how I had ever been mistaken about his identity, even without his beard. His hair was mussed now, and the fancy moustache drooped on one side, but he didn't look any less menacing.

He saw me and stopped, astonished. "You!" he snarled, "It was you, was it, pointed me out to the law? I should have done away with you while I had the chance."

I didn't speak. He came closer, bending down so

that his face was only inches from mine. "I'll be free again one of these days, Master Percy, sooner than you think. Then I'll come after you! We have a score to settle, you and I — a large score!"

"Enough of that, Barry. Leave the lad alone, now. He's just been doing his duty." The constable gestured with his revolver and Barry moved slowly away, his eyes still on my face.

"Don't you be forgetting now, young Percy! Don't you forget James Barry, for he will never forget *you*!" He laughed, softly.

"'To the kitchen, Barry. Move now." The two of them, followed by the tollkeeper, went into the kitchen. Judging by the sounds coming from there, Constable Sullivan was adding extra bonds to his captive and Barry didn't care for it much. "There. That ought to hold you until the stage comes tomorrow morning," I heard the constable say. "And it will keep you out of my sight, too, you misbegotten murderer!"

"Murderer? We'll let the judge decide that, Constable. You've not one bit of proof against me!"

"We'll see about that, Barry. We'll see." The constable and the tollkeeper came back into the main room, leaving Barry in the kitchen. "He's bound well," said the constable. "He's not going to get loose, or even move much tonight. And I've got his gun and knife."

He looked at me closely. "Don't worry, Ted. He can't hurt you. That was talk, just talk."

I still didn't speak. Constable Sullivan came to me and put a hand on my shoulder, trying to reassure me. Don't worry, Ted," he repeated. "The law and Judge Begbie will take care of him. He's seen his last day of freedom."

I nodded at him, not wanting to trust my voice. "Come, now," he said gently, "let's get you back to bed. There's a few hours of sleep left before the stage arrives." He took my arm and led me to the small bed in the corner. "I'll not be sleeping," he said. "I'll be awake, keeping an eye on him, until he's safely away in a nice strong jail. You can sleep, Ted. You're safe."

I lay down and turned my face to the wall. The constable pulled up a chair and sat facing the kitchen door, gun in hand. The old tollkeeper settled down on his cot and was soon snoring.

Hour after hour went by, until finally the sky began to lighten. I lay there, still awake. I knew then that I, like the constable, would not be able to close my eyes and rest until James Barry was safely locked up.

The stage arrived early the next morning. Mr. Tingley stopped at the tollhouse to see if we had any news. "Will you look at that!" he exclaimed as he caught sight of the handcuffed Barry. "I see we have an extra passenger on the trip home! Nice work, men!"

Barry and Constable Sullivan boarded the stage, Barry's handcuffs being fastened to the edge of the wooden seat so that he could barely move. "In you go, Ted," said the constable. "We're off."

I looked at Mr. Tingley. He nodded, understanding. "I think the boy would prefer to ride up front with me," he said, "away from the monster we're carrying."

I smiled at him, relieved. I didn't think I could bear the thought of sitting next to James Barry for the long trip home. "If I may, Mr. Tingley?" I said.

"Sure, son. All the way home if you like."

Because the stage was carrying a wanted criminal, all the other passengers were dropped off at the next road-house to wait for tomorrow's stage. We went on alone. Our rest stops were shortened and the fastest team of horses brought for us at each change. We made the journey home in thirty hours of actual travelling time, almost half the time it had taken us to get to the bridge! I stayed beside Mr. Tingley all the way, refusing his offers of licorice. I couldn't eat. I couldn't even eat at any of the rest stops. I didn't sleep, either. None of us did. We didn't stop anywhere long enough to put our heads down, even for a few minutes.

I arrived home exhausted, pale, with large black circles under my eyes. Pa took one look at me, then lifted me off the driver's box. "It's to bed with you, son," he said. "But first a bowl of hot soup."

"Pa — he — I —"

"Shh. No need to talk about it. I understand."

We pushed our way through the large crowd that had gathered, eager to catch a glimpse of the man who was suspected of murdering Charles Blessing. The jail was just behind the courthouse, and Chief Constable Fitzgerald was helping Constable Sullivan escort their prisoner to it. I looked back and saw Barry between the two of them, standing tall, almost proudly. He lifted his head and, through the crowd, caught sight of me.

"Remember, young Percy," he called. "I'll be coming for you just as soon as I get free. Don't you forget James Barry!"

Pa pulled me close to him. "He'll be safely locked up in a few minutes now," he said. "You have no cause to worry."

We turned our backs on the crowd and on James Barry, and slowly started walking home.

13

Interlude

J ames Barry was not to stay long in the Richfield jail.
There was a preliminary hearing at which it was
decided that there was enough evidence against him
for him to stand trial for the murder of Charles Morgan
Blessing. However, the trial could not be held until July,
when Judge Begbie would be making his next annual trip
to the gold fields to hear cases.

Our small jail was not meant to hold murderers — only
the occasional drunk miner or suspected claim jumper. It
wasn't large enough or secure enough to hold a probable
murderer for any length of time. Consequently, Barry was
taken to the larger, more secure prison in New Westminster.

Once he was out of town I relaxed a bit. I tried to forget
about him and about the way his face looked when he told
me he had a score to settle with me. I almost succeeded.

Life in Barkerville returned to normal. Moses's shop
continued to do good business — he was an excellent barber after all — but no longer did people line up outside
for a chance to talk to him about Charles Blessing and
the gold nugget stickpin. I went back to my books and to

my music lessons with Mr. Malanion. Ma got me fed and rested to her heart's content, and let me return to my habit of wandering the town in the afternoons.

Fall became winter. The snow fell and Williams Creek froze solid. A few hardy miners continued to work their deep shafts, cursing at the cold and the ice. Someone was found frozen stiff in his cabin. He was one of the unfortunate ones whose luck, grub, and firewood had all run out at the same time. Christmas came and went with much merriment and high spirits on the Creek. Finally, winter gave up its firm hold and the first signs of spring began to appear.

I turned thirteen that spring. Pa took a good, hard look at me and announced that all that book learning was fine, but I needed a trade as well, and it was high time I got myself one. I began to spend part of each afternoon in the carpentry shop with him, learning his skills. I grew to love the feel of freshly sanded wood, the rich smells of sawdust and glue, and the glow of pride I had when I earned my pa's praise. "You've got the hands of a craftsman, Ted," he told me. "You've a natural talent there. Now, let's get to work on the things you can learn to help that talent along."

Summer came, taking its time as it always does in the Cariboo. The house filled up with the smells of huckleberry jam, wild strawberry preserves and Saskatoon jelly as Ma boiled and stirred, laying in a stock of sweetness against the next winter.

My boots and overalls suddenly seemed too small. Over the winter and spring I had grown almost three inches. I was taller than Moses now, and we both laughed about it. "Looks as if you're going to grow into that big name of yours, Ted," he said one day. I was busier, too, and what with helping Pa in his shop as well as keeping up with my studies, I spent less time with Moses. But we were still friends, still close.

I had almost forgotten about James Barry. True, I did have nightmares once in a while when I would awaken, drenched with sweat, to find my parents beside my bed. "You were screaming again, son" they'd say. "Are you all right?"

"Another dream that's all," I'd tell them. "Just another dream." Then I'd lie there, unable to sleep until I saw the first light of dawn. I never did tell them what I was dreaming about, but I think they knew. I never spoke of James Barry and his coming trial — not to Moses, not to my parents, not to anyone.

One afternoon, late in July, the stage pulled up at the express office across from the barbershop, and a tall figure stepped out. He had a full head of hair, a well-waxed moustache, and a grey beard with a broad streak of black down the centre. Chief Constable Fitzgerald greeted him respectfully, and the two of them went off to the House Hotel together.

I was in Moses's shop, watching out the window. "Moses ..." I called. He came to look.

"Ah! Judge Begbie is here. Court will be in session soon, I reckon."

I shivered. That meant that James Barry would be returning to the small jail at Richfield to stand trial. Since Judge Begbie would be on the bench, Barry would have a fair hearing. Begbie was known for his passion for justice, as well as his strictness where law and order was concerned.

James Barry was brought back. The Richfield jail had been cleaned and made more secure for his arrival, and a constable was to stay on guard there, day and night. My nightmares increased, once Barry was back in town, but during the day I usually managed to put all thoughts of the coming trial out of my head. What was going to happen would have nothing to do with me. It would be up to Judge Begbie, the jury, and the law to decide Barry's fate. My part was over, finished.

The days crept by, the trial date drawing closer and closer. Barkerville seemed almost to hold its breath with excitement as it waited. I waited anxiously, too.

14

The Trial

The day of Barry's trial the Richfield courthouse was packed to overflowing. Long before the arrival of the prisoner or Judge Begbie, the wooden benches were crammed with eager spectators. The first row, right behind the lawyers' table, was reserved for witnesses. I sat in the second row between Ma and Pa.

I hadn't wanted to go to the trial, but my parents had insisted. I think that they wanted me to see James Barry again, see that he was well guarded and unable to escape. My nightmares had been pretty bad lately. I hoped Ma and Pa were right and the dreams of him that troubled me would disappear once I saw him again, saw him securely guarded, well out of my way.

As the jury filed into the courtroom the spectators looked up eagerly, and the whispering and muttering that had filled the tall room stopped. The members of the jury solemnly took their places. They were all men of substance in the community. No one could serve on a jury unless he could prove that he had at least fifty dollars or owned property. These twelve men would listen to the evidence for and against James Barry, and decide on his guilt or innocence. They all looked as if they were taking that responsibility seriously.

There was a gasp from the spectators as Chief Constable Fitzgerald came through the back door. James Barry followed him, and was led to his place in the prisoner's dock. Once inside, Barry's handcuffs were removed. He sat down on the small stool in the dock, and calmly turned to look at the spectators.

I tried to duck behind the head of the person in front of me, but I was too late. As James Barry spotted me, his lips twisted into a cruel smile, and he lifted his hand and waved to me. "Morning, Master Percy," he called. "Remember now ..."

"Quiet, Barry." The chief constable put a restraining hand on Barry's shoulder. No talking!"

Barry kept his peace after that, but I don't think he took his eyes from me during the whole trial. I looked at the judge's bench, and at the elaborate carving that arched over it. I looked at the backs of people's necks, at the lawyers, at the witnesses. But whenever my eyes flickered to the prisoner, James Barry was still watching me. Looking, smiling, thinking ...

The trial took two full days, two unpleasant days. I didn't want to go back the second day, but Constable Sullivan said that I might be called to testify, if they needed someone to support his statement. I spent the two days squirming in my seat, listening to the evidence, trying not to look at James Barry.

There were many witnesses. The packer who had found Charles Blessing's body was first. Someone laughed when he told of following a grouse, hoping for an easy dinner, and all but stepping on the corpse. "I tell you, Yer Honour, I got so derned upset when I saw that thing, Mr. Blessing's body, I mean, lying there that I let the grouse get clean away. Went hungry that night, I can tell you!"

"Silence in the courtroom!" Judge Begbie spoke harshly as he looked down from his raised bench.

"Ladies and Gentlemen. This is a court of law, not a performance at the Theatre Royal. If you cannot restrain yourselves and control these unseemly outbursts I shall have the bailiff clear the courtroom and conduct this trial without benefit of onlookers!"

Everyone was quiet after that, and stayed quiet, too, right through the rest of the testimony.

Moses took the stand, looking as nervous as I felt. He told his story: how he had first met Blessing, then James Barry; how Barry had tried to borrow money from him; how he had never again seen his friend, Charles Blessing, but had recognized the nugget stickpin worn by the prisoner.

"One moment, Mr. Moses," interrupted Judge Begbie. "Is this nugget pin available for inspection?" The nugget was produced for Judge Begbie to look at and then passed to Moses on the judge's instructions.

The judge watched as Moses inspected the pin. "It is necessary to find out if, in fact, it is the same pin that Mr. Moses saw Mr. Blessing wearing."

"Yes, Your Honour. It is the same stickpin, the one Charles showed to me on Cariboo Road, the same one I later saw in James Barry's coat lapel. Charles called it his 'luck' — although it doesn't seem to have brought him much — and it's easy to recognize because of the face in it."

"The face?" The judge was interested in the stickpin and had Moses demonstrate how the face became visible when the nugget was turned upside-down. Judge Begbie held it carefully while he made a quick sketch of it in his trial notebook, then had the pin shown to the jury. Each of them studied it, turning it first one way and then the other until the face became clear, then passed it on to his neighbour.

Other witnesses followed Moses and gave their evidence. A Mr. Stark told of seeing the two of them, Barry and Blessing, together on the road from Quesnel. His testimony was supported by a Mr. Elliot who also saw the two men, this time camped near Pinegrove Creek, on the evening of May 30, 1866. A shudder ran through the courtroom as we all realized that he must have been the last person to see Charles Blessing alive — except for his murderer!

The owner of a lodging house testified that James Barry had taken a room in his house early in June, paying with a twenty-dollar gold piece. He also stated that Barry hadn't seemed to work much, but always had money to spend. After this, Moses was recalled to the witness stand to confirm that James Barry, a few days earlier, had been broke and tried to borrow money from both him and Charles Blessing.

Constable Sullivan's testimony took a long time. He told of finding me tied up in the miner's shack, of what I had told him about Barry's escape plans, and of the trap he had set at the swinging bridge. "It was young Ted identified him for me, Your Honour," he said. "The prisoner would have got clean away if it hadn't of been for Ted."

"Well, Constable, in that case it seems as if this court owes Master Ted its thanks," said Judge Begbie, nodding to me as he spoke. "You have served the law well, Theodore MacIntosh, and we are all grateful."

Everyone in the courtroom turned to look at me. I could feel my ears burning, and hoped I wasn't blushing. There was a moment's silence before the trial continued, and in that silence James Barry spoke, softly but clearly.

"I owe him something, too, Your Honour — but it isn't my thanks!"

15

The Other Side of the Story

There were more witnesses, many more. The lawyers asked questions, the witnesses answered, and Judge Begbie called for more information. The white walls of the large courtroom seemed to reflect the voices back to the spectators who added their quiet murmurings to the sound. It wasn't a loud noise, but it seemed to fill the courtroom like a distant swarm of bees. And, like bees, the words bumbled around and around in my head as I listened to the evidence growing against James Barry. Every witness seemed to have something to say that added to his guilt; words were piling on top of him, closing in on him, smothering him with their weight. Yet he said nothing throughout the long days; just sat, listened, and stared at me.

Finally there were no more witnesses to be called, no more questions to be asked. The courtroom grew completely still while Judge Begbie wrote a final few notes in his trial book. Then he turned to the prisoner.

"We will now hear any statement the accused has to make in his own defence. "You may speak, Mr. Barry."

James Barry rose, faced the judge, and began to talk in a clear, level voice.

"Your Honour, I am not guilty. There has been a terrible mistake made, one which I will try to clear up right now. I never travelled with Charles Blessing at all. We bunked together for one night, but the morning we were to leave Quesnel he said he had sore feet, and I went on alone. The witnesses who claim to have seen me with him on the road are wrong. They saw Charles Blessing with another man, a man who was his murderer!"

He took his eyes from the judge and once again glanced my way before continuing. "Blessing left the place where we bunked before I was packed up. He said he was going to see a doctor about his feet. After he had gone, I found his stickpin near where he had slept. It was that same gold nugget that has caused so much excitement in this court. I took it with me, knowing how much he cherished it. I planned to return it to him as soon as I saw him in Barkerville. I, too, was surprised when he didn't turn up at the Creek within a few days. I was holding the nugget pin in safekeeping, waiting for my chance to give it back to him. After all, he had loaned me money to get started — that very twenty-dollar gold piece that I paid to the owner of the lodging house. The least I could do for him was to look after his luck.

"On my way to Barkerville, I passed two men camping near Pinegrove Creek, but I went further on that night and didn't stop near them. That witness, too, is mistaken when he claims to have seen me and Charles Blessing camped at Pinegrove. I had long since passed the spot, and Mr. Blessing was not travelling with me.

"May I remind your honour and the respected jury, that it was dusk when Mr. Elliot claims to have passed the camp at Pinegrove, and at dusk one's eyes can be tricked by the light. It is easy to mistake one man for another. It was some other man he saw camped there with Charles Blessing, not me."

Again he paused, this time smiling slightly as he looked in my direction. "Now, Your Honour, we come to the unfortunate part of my story. When young Percy here called me a murderer I am afraid that I panicked, which is why I acted in such an unseemly manner towards him. I truly hope he has forgiven me and my rough ways. I never meant to frighten the lad.

"I was afraid that just what *has* happened *would* happen; that Mr. Moses, a man never known for minding his own business, would jump to conclusions regarding me and Mr. Blessing and how I came to have the nugget pin. I thought that suspicion would fall on me, and wishing to avoid any unpleasantness, such as being shut up in jail, I decided to take my leave of Barkerville. I see now that I was wrong. I should have stayed and told my story, as I am telling it now.

"Charles Blessing was a good man. He lent me money and offered to lend me more, should I need it. I found his nugget by accident, and I was never with him on the Quesnel road. I know that Your Honour and you gentlemen of the jury are intelligent and logical men and will understand how a combination of unfortunate circumstances and unreliable witnesses have brought me to stand before you — unjustly!

"I repeat, I am innocent of this charge. I did *not* kill Charles Blessing. God rest his soul. I never saw him again after that morning in Quesnel when his feet were bothering him so. I am sure the facts of my innocence will be obvious to such learned men as yourselves, and you will allow how it has all been a terrible mistake and bring in a verdict of Not Guilty. For indeed, gentlemen, I *am not guilty!*"

He bowed slightly to the jury, and then sat down. No one moved. Even Judge Begbie seemed taken aback by Barry's long speech. He had spoken so reasonably without any of the cruelty he had shown towards me, and appeared to be just what he said he was — an unfortunate man caught in a web of events that made him look guilty.

"Thank you, Mr. Barry." Judge Begbie finally spoke. "I am sure that your statement, which you have presented so eloquently, will be duly considered by the jury."

He spoke to the jury for a few minutes more while going over the evidence that had been heard. Finally he cautioned them. "I must impress on you that if, in your minds, there is a reasonable doubt that it is possible the accused did not commit this murder, then you must return a verdict of Not Guilty and allow him his freedom."

The twelve men nodded their heads, and at a signal from the bailiff, rose and filed out of the room. Judge Begbie returned to his chambers. The spectators stood, stretched, and began to talk to their neighbours. All around me I could hear discussion about Barry's testimony. It had sounded so logical, so sensible, so reasonable. Perhaps it had happened just the way he told it; perhaps he *was* innocent.

But then — why had he tied me up, held his gun to my head, and threatened me after he had been caught? Why did he tell Moses the stickpin was *his?* And why didn't he tell his story at once, instead of waiting until he stood before the Judge and jury?

I couldn't really believe that he was innocent. Somewhere deep inside me I knew, positively knew, that he had murdered Charles Blessing.

But if the jury believed him, they would have to set him free. Free to come and settle his score with me!

16

The Verdict

It took the jury only one hour to decide whether James Barry was guilty or innocent. They filed back into the courtroom, looking even more serious than they had at the beginning of the trial. James Barry was led in and once again placed in the prisoner's dock. The spectators, many of whom had gone outside to stretch their legs, rushed back to their seats, some barely reaching their places before the bailiff announced, "All rise," when Judge Begbie entered the courtroom from his chambers.

"Gentlemen of the jury," he asked, "Have you reached a verdict?"

"We have, Your Honour," answered the foreman, his voice low.

"Then kindly inform the court of that verdict. And please, speak up." The judge settled back in his large, carved chair, waiting.

I held my breath. There wasn't a sound to be heard in the crowded courtroom — not a rustle, not a voice, not a breath.

The foreman of the jury cleared his throat. "We find the prisoner Guilty, Your Honour," he said. "Guilty as charged," he repeated.

A deep sigh swept through the room, as if everyone there had released his breath at the same instant. Then movement began again. Heads turned, bodies shifted, and all eyes focused on James Barry.

Judge Begbie stood. "James Barry, this court has found you guilty of the murder of Charles Morgan Blessing on May 31, 1866. I am in complete accord with their decision. I, personally, can no more doubt your guilt than if I had been an eyewitness to it. I have no doubt that you persuaded your victim to leave the road and then perpetrated the crime; and that you did it for the sake of profit, the most sordid of motives. You have dyed your hands in blood ... The law claims a death for a death."

He slowly placed a square of black silk over his long wig before speaking again. "My painful duty now is to pass the last sentence of the law on you, which is that you be taken to jail whence you came, and from there to a public place of execution, there to be hanged by the neck until you are dead."

He carefully removed the black silk square, then turned and left the bench, his long robes billowing out behind him. He paused briefly in front of the prisoner's dock, looked at James Barry, shook his head almost sadly, then left the room. Constable Sullivan and Chief Constable Fitzgerald replaced the handcuffs on Barry who sat silent, looking as if he had been hit in the stomach. As they pulled him to his feet and began to lead him towards the door, towards his cell, he stopped and appealed to them. "But I'm innocent! Constable, you must believe me. I'm innocent!"

"Come along now, Barry" said Constable Sullivan. "If the judge and the jury have found you guilty, then guilty you are — as if we all didn't know it long ago."

James Barry's eyes searched the courtroom until he saw me. "Master Percy, tell them!" he called. "Tell them I'm innocent. I could have killed you when I had the chance, but I spared your life. Would a murderer have done that? Tell them how I spared you; tell them I'm innocent!"

I said nothing, but sat and watched as he was pulled, none too gently, from the room.

From outside the courtroom I heard his voice, faintly, "I meant no harm to you, Ted. Tell them, tell them ..."

I never saw him alive again.

17

A Life for a Life

August 8, 1867. The day James Barry was to die. The sky was blue, cloudless, and the sun beat down, warming the earth that would soon cover his body.

Barkerville was in a tremendous state of excitement. There had never been an execution on the Creek. People talked of nothing else all day, and the town was divided right down the middle — into those who planned to attend the hanging, and those who planned to do anything but!

My parents belonged to the last group. They said that they had no intention of watching a man die before their eyes, and I was strictly instructed to stay away too. "Any man, even a convicted murderer, deserves to die with dignity," said Pa. "Making a public spectacle of his death takes that away from him. This family, at least, will let him die without standing around like hungry coyotes watching a sick rabbit. Mind now, you stay away from the Richfield courthouse this evening, Ted."

I had no intention of going. James Barry's speech to the court had upset me, upset me to the point where I was no longer sure of his guilt. He had sounded so reasonable, his story had seemed so logical, and he hadn't shown any of the evil that I had sensed in him earlier. Maybe he hadn't murdered Charles Blessing. Maybe the verdict was wrong.

The hanging was to take place that evening, at six o'clock. The scaffold had been built, and crowds had gathered just to watch it going up. According to the law, the scaffold had to be dismantled immediately after the execution. I had heard from Moses that the men responsible for taking it down had been accepting offers of money, money in exchange for a piece of wood on which a man had died! The thought made me sick.

I didn't do much that day. I sat in Moses's shop for a while, but neither of us had anything to say. We were both busy with our own thoughts. We didn't dare talk about James Barry's statement. Both of us had done all we could to see him arrested and tried; neither of us could face the thought that he might, after all, be innocent.

Later, I went home and took out my violin. Although I practiced for two hours, I couldn't keep my mind on what I was doing, and my fingers refused to co-operate. Finally I put the violin aside and went down to the carpentry shop to see if Pa needed me. For a while, working with the clean wood, feeling the rough texture of sandpaper in my hands, and watching the shavings curl away from the plane, I almost forgot what was to happen that evening. Almost, but not quite.

Dinner was quiet. My parents left at about half past five. There was a special church service that evening, scheduled for the time of the hanging. Many people were going to the service. They were mostly those who didn't approve of the public execution. I guess they planned on praying for James Barry's soul. I didn't want to go. I just wanted to get this long day over with, over and forgotten.

"Are you sure you don't want to change your mind and come with us?" asked Ma as she tied on her bonnet. "You won't be worried, staying alone right now?"

"No, Ma." I managed a small smile. "I'll be all right. It's over now, you know. All over."

"Well, we'll be going, then. You could split a load of wood for the cookstove. We're running low," said Pa. Then they were gone, and I was alone.

*

I planned on splitting the wood. I went outside, sharpened the axe, and even took a few swings with it. But then I turned, and started up the hill, drawn towards Richfield, towards the hanging.

I don't know what I was thinking. I didn't want to see James Barry hanged, but I did want to know for sure that he was dead, that he could never come back and settle his score with me. Maybe I halfway expected that he wouldn't be hanged, that there would be a last minute stay of execution. Perhaps the jury had reconsidered — could a jury do that? I didn't know. All I knew was that I had to find out what was happening. So I walked up the hill, towards the newly built gallows.

Long before I reached the courthouse I could hear the crowd. Voices reached down the trail to me, almost as if they were urging me to hurry. I kept walking, wondering why the last few yards seemed so steep today. Then I rounded a corner, and the tall, white building was in front of me.

The crowd must have been fifty thick in some places. I knew the scaffold was there, but I couldn't see it. It was completely surrounded by people. There were people perched in the trees, standing on rocks, and pressing closely around the front of the courthouse.

I turned around again. I didn't want to watch, anyway. I found a large pine tree, just off the path, and sat down with my back to it. I could hear the crowd, hear them laughing and pushing and shuffling their feet, but I couldn't see anything.

I waited, and listened.

The crowd gasped and a voice called out, "There he is! There's the murderer!" The noise grew louder. It seemed that everyone had a comment to make.

"Doesn't he look dreadful?"

"I heard that he's been sick."

"Sick my foot! That's the face of a guilty conscience."

"Oh, look! There's a priest with him."

"Hope he's said his prayers, not that they'll do him any good where he's going!"

Silence fell, and then a single voice, I don't know whose, echoed down to me. "James Barry, have you any last words to say before you go to meet your maker?"

The silence returned, silence so deep that the rustle of the leaves in the big cottonwood trees outside the courthouse sounded loud and out of place.

"I am innocent. You are killing an innocent man." There was no mistaking Barry's voice. It rose above the crowd, clear and loud. "God rest *your* souls," he continued, "for I am innocent of this deed."

A murmur ran through the crowd. I heard a few snatches of conversation, "Not likely ... did you hear that, innocent as a killer wolf ... the man's a liar." Then all was quiet again.

In the silence, the absolute quiet that had come over the spectators, a sudden loud crash rang out — the sound of a heavy trap door falling and crashing against its supports. As one, the crowd sighed.

It was done.

It Ends — Perhaps

"Ted!" the voice was loud and came from behind me. I jumped and turned around. Moses stood on the trail, looking at me.

"Ted. I met your ma and pa in town. They said you were home alone, so I thought I'd come up and stay with you. I figured you could do with some company right now. I know *I* didn't want to be alone this evening."

"I just ..."

"Your pa said that on no account were you to go to the hanging, but when I found your house empty I knew where you would be. Why, Ted, why?"

"Oh, Moses." I suddenly found it hard to speak. I swallowed, and went on. "I don't know why. I wasn't going to come to the hanging, really I wasn't. It just — happened."

Moses left the road and came to sit down beside me. A few people began to drift away from the crowd. One lady was crying. The rest of them stayed, watching.

"He's dead, Moses," I said. "I heard the noise as the trap fell. He's dead."

"Yes. He won't be troubling you again, Ted."

"But he's dead! They killed him."

"We killed him, Ted. The law is ours, the people's. It does things in our name, to protect us and keep us safe."

"But Moses, the law — we — have no right to take a man's life."

He sighed. "Ted, it's just punishment for what he did to my friend Charles. An eye for an eye — and a life for a life. It's justice."

"No, Moses, it isn't. It isn't right!" I put my head between my hands. I was shaking, shaking right down to my toes, and the palms of my hands were sweating. I hoped I wasn't going to cry.

"It isn't right," I said again, my voice muffled. "He spared my life. He didn't shoot me when he had the chance. And I ..." I swallowed hard again. "I helped to kill him, Moses!"

Moses reached out a hand and put it on my shoulder. "You did what you had to do, Ted. You helped the law, helped me, helped all of us. You aren't responsible for his death. He is. James Barry is responsible for his own death because he took the life of a fellow man."

"Are we sure, Moses? When you listened to him talking in the courtroom, were you *sure* that he was guilty?"

Moses thought for a while before he answered. "No, Ted, I guess we can never be absolutely sure that he wasn't telling the truth. But the judge and jury didn't believe him; they found him guilty. He spoke well, but the evidence was against him."

"Moses, what if he is ... *was* innocent? What if we hanged an innocent man?"

"That is the trouble with hanging, Ted. You can't change your mind, and say 'We made a mistake, sorry.' I believe he was guilty, though. In my heart I knew that he was guilty, that he murdered my friend in cold blood."

"I hope your heart is right, Moses. I hope it's telling you the truth."

Moses stood up and looked down at me, smiling slightly. "I'm sure of it, Ted. James Barry was guilty."

I stood, too. "But still, even if he was guilty, we didn't have the right to murder him in return. What we did, what the law did, is as wrong as what he did."

"Perhaps, Ted, perhaps." Moses began to walk down the trail. I walked with him, slowly.

"Right or wrong, it's the law, Ted. Maybe someday they'll change it. Maybe sometime in the future they'll figure out what to do with evil men, with murderers, without killing them in return."

We went on in silence. Dusk was growing thicker, and the night sounds of the gold fields began to make themselves heard — the slow croak of frogs, the sleepy noises of birds settling down for the night, the gurgling, splashing of the creek itself. We reached my house and stopped.

"Your ma and pa aren't back yet," said Moses, noticing the dark windows. "I shouldn't mention where you've been tonight, if I were you."

"No, I won't."

"Do you want me to come in with you?"

"No, I'll be all right, Moses. Thank you. I guess I never thought much about what they'd do to him, to Barry, if they found him guilty. I never thought that he would have to pay with his life — that I would help to send a man to his death."

Moses spoke softly. "It's over now, Ted. It's over."

We looked at each other in silence for a while. Moses finally sighed and spoke, "Well, I'll be going, then. Come and visit with me when you're not busy in your pa's shop."

"I will, Moses, I will."

He walked away, down the trail, a slender, dark figure almost invisible in the growing dusk. Suddenly he stopped, turning back towards me. "Remember, Ted," he called, "it's over. He's gone. You'll sleep easier from now on."

I wonder. I wonder if I will.

Acknowledgements

The author wishes to thank the following people for their help and encouragement: W.G. Quackenbush, Curator, Barkerville Historic Town; Michael Rawluk; Kim Herdman; Alvin Sanders; Ron Young; Teacher Librarian Maria Lepetitch; and the students of 150 Mile School.

Historical Notes

This book is fictionalized history. All characters and most events are factual, with the exception of my hero, Ted, and his family. Therefore, although James Barry did hang for the murder of Charles Morgan Blessing, it is unlikely that he was ever involved with a twelve-year-old boy.

This story was difficult to write because of the many versions of the Blessing murder that exist. In one version the nugget was reported to look like an angel; in other versions, a man's face or a skull. Similarly, the discovery of the nugget is told in many ways. One story says that Barry gave it to a saloon girl who tried to pay Moses with it, a second that Moses saw someone else wearing it, and yet another that Moses himself recognized it while shaving Barry. Barry was captured either at Yale or at the Alexandra suspension bridge; again, it depends on which book you read. I took parts of each story to write this book, which is why, if you read another version of the Blessing murder, some things may be told differently.

Some of my material comes directly from the *Cariboo Sentinel*, Barkerville's paper, some from the files in the Barkerville "Curatorial Service," some from talking to people who have studied this era, and a great deal from various history books.

I have taken liberties with the setting of the story. Barkerville, in its entirety, burned down in September of 1868, and what visitors see today is a reconstruction of the new town. The events in this story occurred in 1866 and 1867, but I have used Barkerville after the fire — specifically, reconstructed Barkerville — as my setting. That Barkerville is what can be seen by any visitor today, and places in the town mentioned in this story are easily recognized.

Similarly, the Richfield Courthouse was not built until 1882, years after James Barry was sentenced and hanged. However, I have chosen again to use the setting that is there now, rather than describing the small building that served as a courthouse until 1882. The new courthouse still stands, and is well worth the mile long uphill hike to see it. An actor portraying Judge Begbie holds court there during the summer session for anyone willing to take the steep walk

Characters

Wellington Delaney Moses

Wellington (or Washington, as some books refer to him) Moses was sometimes known as The Barkerville Barber. He died in 1890, and was most probably buried in the Barkerville cemetery in one of the many unmarked graves that still exist. His role in the story is accurate, with the exception of his friendship with Ted. His barbershop, the one now on display in Barkerville, wasn't actually built until 1879. However, he did have a shop in the town before the fire, and he did keep a diary, samples of which may be seen outside his shop today. His hair restorer, which he made himself from a secret formula, was famous throughout the gold fields.

Charles Morgan Blessing

Very little, only that which Moses could report, is known about Charles Morgan Blessing. I have included almost everything I could find out about him in this story. He did own the strangely-shaped nugget stickpin, but his story about it being his "luck" is my own invention.

James Barry

Not too much is known about James Barry, either. However, I did find one quote that stated he looked like "a tall, hard-faced Texan." Another source thought that he was Irish. His statement to the jury is my own invention; nowhere could I find any record of his having explained how he came to have Charles Blessing's nugget stickpin, or in any way defending himself against the charge of murder. However, he did repeat, over and over, that he was innocent. He was hanged on August 8, 1867, at six in the morning. (For dramatic reasons I have changed the time in this story to six in the evening.) No one knows for sure just where he was buried. Another man was tried and hanged at the same time, but information about him and whom he murdered is very scanty. He has no part in this story, so I have left him out. He and James Barry were the only two men ever hanged in the Williams Creek area.

James Barry was convicted mainly on the testimony that I have included in this book. No one, not even Judge Begbie, whose summing up I have slightly paraphrased, seemed to have any doubt as to his guilt. However, as I researched this story, I began to have doubts. It seems to me that a good modern trial lawyer could have saved him from the gallows; the evidence against him was all circumstantial and much depended on Moses's testimony. But James Barry is definitely the villain of this story, and I leave it to the reader to decide if the jury was correct in its decision.

Mr. Malanion

Ted's music teacher, Mr. J.B. Malanion, was a violinist who had played in the Paris Opera. He taught music in Barkerville, but his main income was from carpentry. His grave can be seen in the Barkerville cemetery.

Madame Bendixen

Madame Fannie Bendixen brought the first hurdy-gurdy girls to Barkerville in 1866. She was their chaperone or protector, as the hurdies were very often young German girls, lacking knowledge of English, and not very sophisticated. The hurdies were dancing girls, and were of "high moral character," unlike many of the saloon girls who provided a different type of entertainment.

Constable Sullivan

Many officers of the law were involved with James Barry, but as Sullivan was the one who actually made the arrest, I chose to use him throughout. Most sources claim that he arrested Barry at Yale after telegraphing to the police there — the first recorded use of the telegraph in British Columbia police history. His trip back by stagecoach was made in record time. One report does use the story of the arrest at the swinging bridge at Alexandra, rather than at Yale. Other than his connection with James Barry, very little is known about him.

Stephen Tingley

Stephen Tingley drove Barnard's stagecoaches for over thirty years beginning with the return journey of the first four-horse stage from Yale to Soda Creek in 1864. The information about the stages and travelling time is correct, but I have no idea whether or not Mr. Tingley was partial to licorice.

Judge Begbie

Sir Matthew Baillie Begbie was the first judge in British Columbia and travelled throughout the territory hearing cases. His title, The Hanging Judge, came not so much from his harshness in dispensing justice, but from his sharp tongue which he used freely on juries, witnesses, and criminals alike. He was a judge for thirty-six uninterrupted years during which time thirty-seven defendants were sentenced to hang. Twenty-six executions actually took place over those years. Many books claim that Begbie's sternness and fairness were the main reasons that law and order was maintained in the gold fields, and one miner is reported to have said of him, "He was the biggest man, the smartest man, the best-looking man, and the damnedest man that ever came over the Cariboo Road.

When he died, in 1894, he was Chief Justice of British Columbia.

Blessing's Grave

Pinegrove Creek, where the murder occurred, is a few miles east of present-day Wingdam, or just before Troll Mountain ski resort. Blessing's grave is well marked as a stop of interest. Parks workers who were resetting the headstone a few years ago inadvertently dug too deeply and found a long, human bone which they hastily replaced. Thus, we know for sure that Charles Blessing (or someone) is, in fact, buried there.

For more information about her Barkerville books, visit Ann's website, annwalsh.ca.